"Having trouble?"

Twisting around in her seat, Cass saw a horse and rider trotting toward her. Jake Munro! He was the last person she wanted to see, but it was too late to start her engine and pull out.

She cursed the blush she could feel spreading up her face. "No."

"I saw you driving out of Sky View."

"Yes," she said, determined not to be daunted by his sheer masculinity. "I've just rented a cottage from your dad."

There was an icy glint in his blue eyes, but she held his gaze without faltering. "Don't worry, though–it's well away from the farm, so you won't have to see me."

He swung his mount away. "It makes no difference to me where you live."

The angry set of his jaw belied his pronouncement, and Cass found herself hoping he wouldn't give poor Bill a hard time.

"Look," she called after him, "I needed somewhere to stay, and your dad had the perfect place."

Jake reined in. The grey mare tossed her beautiful head, and foam flew like snowflakes.

"I already told you," he repeated drily, "it means nothing to me where you live."

But as he rode away, Cass couldn't help watching. Man and horse, moving as one.

Dear Reader,

I truly believe that we all have a soul mate somewhere out there.

If you find your kindred spirit then never let go. Real love is well worth fighting for. No matter what.

I do hope you enjoy reading this story as much as I have enjoyed writing it.

Be happy,

Eleanor

HARLEQUIN HEARTWARMING

Eleanor Jones

The Country Vet

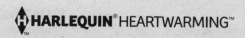

Recycling programs
for this product may
not exist in your area.

ISBN-13: 978-0-373-36676-7

THE COUNTRY VET

Copyright © 2014 by Eleanor Grace Jones

Printed in U.S.A.

HARLEQUIN®
www.Harlequin.com

ELEANOR JONES

Born and raised on a farm in Northern England, Eleanor Jones has always had a passion for animals and the countryside. She has been writing almost all her life. The poems and stories she wrote as a child, which still grace a cupboard somewhere, were mostly written in longhand. She later wrote articles for an equestrian magazine and her first big break came when she began writing teenage pony mystery stories. These still sell successfully in seven countries throughout Europe and in North America.

Married at eighteen to Peter, she had two children and then set up the Holmescales Riding Centre in Cumbria with her husband. This busy center now trains career students, takes hacks and treks and teaches at all levels from children and total novices to competition riders.

Eleanor still rides every day, schooling and training horses, and her daughter is now a partner in the business and competes at the national level. Her son is married with two children, and she loves to spend as much time with them as she can.

I dedicate this book to all those who love
animals and the countryside.

All the best,

Eleanor

CHAPTER ONE

JAKE SETTLED EASILY into the saddle, picking up the reins with a confidence born of hours on horseback. Beneath him Carlotta sidled, snorting and shaking her head, sensing her master's mood and anticipating what she knew was to come. She needed no aid to urge her forward as he turned his eyes, as always, toward the skyline.

There was something about the vast infinity of the sky that made a strange kind of sense to Jake, when it seemed that there was little sense in life anymore. The way the bleak, ancient mass of the fell met the sky's glorious, timeless canopy, made him feel somehow insignificant, a mere dot in the march of time. He liked insignificance.

The mare's hooves echoed in his ears as his mind spilled over with memories— memories that flooded out from their confinement, painful and raw. A whole year, twelve long, endless months, and the accident still felt as fresh as it had on the day it happened. Every morning, when he awoke from yet another restless night, he went through the motions, working as hard as he could, talking, smiling, eating—and yet all he felt inside was sadness. The only time he felt even half alive these days was when he was riding.

Asking Carlotta to canter, Jake threw caution to the wind, gathering her up to jump the gate. She rose willingly beneath him, landing effortlessly on the tough grass and galloping up the steep slope of the fell. He leaned forward against her neck, feeling her power beneath him, trying to live in the moment and push all the memories aside. Tara's cold eyes, the confusion in Robbie's; his mother, warm and vibrant... and Lucy, dear little Lucy.

THE CALL CAME in just as Cass was on her way back to the surgery—as the golden, late-summer sun slipped slowly behind the dark mass of the Lakeland hills.

Her first day at the Low Fell Animal Clinic had proved to be a challenge, to say the least, and it seemed that it wasn't over yet. She forced an image of the irate, red-faced farmer in his muck-splattered overalls, bellowing like one of his bulls, firmly to the back of her mind. "Cass here," she responded. "What have you got for me?"

Sally's clear voice filled Cass's car, her tone clipped and urgent. "We have an emergency…a horse…at Jake Munro's place. Jake usually insists on having Donald, but he's miles away. Where are you now?"

Cass glanced around at the rugged countryside.

"I don't really have a clue, but I'm just leaving Fell Side Farm, if that's any help…"

"That's great, you must be nearby. Carry on down the hill toward the village and take your first left up a narrow lane. You can't miss it. You'll see the sign on your right—Sky View."

The sun finally vanished, and long, shadowy fingers fell across the road ahead. Cass headed down the hill, peering over her steering wheel. "What's the problem, anyway?"

"Sounds like colic. The guy who rang

in, Jake Munro's dad, Bill, seems to think it's serious."

"Okay." Cass blinked, trying to focus her over-stretched brain on the task ahead. "I'll be there as fast as I can."

The narrow lane crept, ribbonlike, around the steep hillside, down toward the dark, shimmering lake far below. She increased her speed as much as she dared, standing on the brakes as amber eyes glowed eerily in the road ahead and breathing a sigh of relief when a flock of sheep scattered in front of her car.

Down in the valley, lights were beginning to twinkle, bright pinpoints in the distance, homes where families were gathering after a busy day, smiling, communicating. Families! Cass felt suffocated as she thought about her own family. It seemed ages since she'd seen her parents, Tim and Molly. Her mother had rung just last night to tell her about the lump she'd found in her breast. It was benign, which was of course a huge relief, but the fact that she hadn't even told her about it until it was all over had upset Cass.

She knew why her mum had kept quiet,

of course, and it was so typical. "I didn't want to worry you if it wasn't really necessary," she'd insisted.

But what if it *had* been necessary, Cass wondered, and she hadn't been there to support her mother. For the last few years, all she'd thought about was her career, endlessly studying for the next exam and eventually trying to get a job. Now she had a job, a good job, so surely she should have a chance to stop and reflect, to spend time with her parents. But she was still thinking about herself and trying to get ahead. She had only just started at Low Fell Animal Clinic, but she already knew she wanted to specialize in horses.

Had she been selfish in her single-minded quest to become a vet? she asked herself, shifting down the gears. The answer sprang easily to her mind as an image of her mother's face settled into place, her tired blue eyes filled with love and kindness. Her mother was always working and always worrying about her only child.

Yes, Cass realized with a lurch of guilt, she *had* been selfish, yet she knew her parents would not have had it any other way.

She had arrived in the world as an afterthought, disrupting their world when they'd both turned forty. Fitting in a baby around running the busy village store her parents had bought when they were first married had been quite a feat, according to Molly. Cass had spent most of her early years in a corner near the vegetables, first in a pram and later in a playpen.

Cass's heart twisted as she thought about her mother's recent health scare. The diagnosis could have been serious, and she wouldn't have known. And Cass bet her mum would have barely taken a day off work. Her parents loved running the store, though. Their customers were their friends, and there was nothing Molly and Tim liked better than to pass the time of day with them, bragging a little about how well *she* was doing. So at least she'd done that for them. She sighed, peering at her surroundings. At least she'd made them proud.

The sign appeared suddenly, jumping out at her from around a curve in the lane and jerking her from her reverie. Sky View Stables was boldly written in an arc above the noble head of a black horse. Cass spun the wheel and swung her hatchback down the gravel drive, suddenly apprehensive about what she might find here.

BILL MUNRO PULLED at his whiskered chin. Why did it have to be Rosie, and where the hell was Jake? He had found the little chestnut pony out in the far meadow. She was in a bad way, sweating and kicking her belly, her head covered with cuts where she'd been thrashing on the ground. He had tried to ring Jake, of course, but got no signal, so he'd called the vet before managing to persuade the reluctant pony back to the yard. He had settled her down in a deep bed of straw, but it seemed that all the fight had left her. That was what worried him most—her despondency. He'd seen the signs before, and it didn't look good.

Car wheels crunched on the gravel. The throb of an engine sputtered and died as the vehicle slithered to a stop. Bill ran out into the yard, waving his arms.

"Over here!"

CASS CLIMBED FROM her car with controlled urgency, reaching for her bag and breathing deeply to slow the heavy beating of her heart. This was her job and she was well trained to do it. She turned toward the old man, noting the fear and panic in his blue eyes, and took control of the situation as professionalism kicked in. Her voice sounded firm and calm in her ears, as if she was watching herself from afar. "Right, now tell me the symptoms clearly and slowly."

"It's Rosie," the man responded, already heading off across the yard. "She's bad. Been like that a long time, I think."

Cass followed hurriedly, running the procedure in her mind.

The pony was standing with its head lowered, sides heaving and a dead look in its eye. Cass's heart sank—twisted gut in its final stages. She went through the motions, checking the pony's heart rate and respiration and trying to ease her pain, knowing in her heart that it was already too late.

"Are you the owner?"

Bill Munro's face was gray, his response stilted. "She belongs to…my son."

Cass looked at him, her hand upturned

in a gesture of helplessness. "I think you know she's in a bad way. I doubt she'd make it to surgery, even if you wanted to try."

"Twisted gut?"

She nodded sadly. "I've seen it before in old ponies. It could be a bit of fatty tissue that's twisted itself around the gut. Surgery is always an option, but it has to be fast, and to be honest…"

Bill finished the sentence for her. "You don't really believe it would be worth putting her through it,"

Cass nodded again, placing a comforting hand on his arm. "I am so sorry."

Bill pulled out his phone, dialing Jake for the twentieth time. No signal. He thrust it back in his pocket, making the decision. "Just do it."

"You're giving me permission to euthanize her?"

"Yes…. Don't worry. I'll take the rap."

Cass's heart ran cold as she looked at the pretty little chestnut mare whose eyes were dull now with pain and fatigue, her sides straining with the effort to breathe. Cass brushed her hand across her eyes. This wasn't why she'd trained to become a vet. Her quest was to save life, not end it. She drew the drug into a syringe, automatically tapping out the air bubbles, searching for a vein. She met no resistance from the exhausted pony.

JAKE STAYED OUT on the hillside as the sun sank slowly downward, lighting the sky with red and gold. Carlotta trotted, eager for home, and he let out a heavy sigh, turning her face back down the steep slope as darkness settled around them.

No matter how bad he felt inside, there were still horses waiting to be fed and chores to do. Life went on remorselessly, and he knew that he would, too—what else was there to do? He'd coped for the past year and he would cope for the next, and the one after that, going through the motions of his empty existence while always believing that if he'd dealt with things a bit better after Tara left, then his mum and Lucy would still be here. His life would still have meaning, and they'd all have a future together.

Jake saw the car as Carlotta jogged sideways through the gate into Sky View. A hatchback, dark green, abandoned in the center of the yard. He reined in, leaping to the ground and drawing the reins over the mare's head in one smooth, easy movement. Who was here, and what did they want? The gray mare ran eagerly into her stall, diving into her hay net as soon as he removed her bridle.

"I'll come back and brush you in a bit," he told her, sliding home the door bolt and depositing her tack on the ground before striding toward the car.

Rosie's stall door was ajar, he noted with a sudden jolt of alarm, peering into the sweet-smelling darkness of her empty stall. Voices trickled over from across the yard. There was someone in the barn. A light shone through the half-open door, casting a glow into the evening gloom and bringing a glisten of gold to the feathers of the ruddy-brown chicken that squawked its displeasure at being disturbed. What was going on? He hesitated, suddenly afraid of what he might find in the barn.

She materialized as if by magic, sleek dark hair and pale skin, staring at him with fathomless brown eyes. He sensed her pain, felt it even before she spoke, and for one endless moment she seemed so familiar, so vulnerable, that his every instinct was to just hold out his arms. When she stepped toward him, holding his gaze, her eyes shone with what looked like unshed tears. Something tore at the numb place in his heart and he froze, raising his barriers as her dark eyes slid away from his. There was no room in his life for compassion anymore, or any other emotion for that matter—only the raw anger that was his constant companion.

Her voice was soft and gentle, caring. "I am so, so sorry."

The beam of light from the barn fell across his foot. He stared at it, watching the dust dance within its confines before glancing back at the girl.

"There was nothing else I could do."

"I gave her permission." His father stepped into view, jaw set and eyes shadowed with grief. Jake pushed past him, his heart already hitting his boots.

Rosie lay motionless on the soft sweet hay. Her eyes were already glazed. He dropped to his knees, stroking her face. The pain he had tried to block out rushed back in one tumultuous wave of grief, erupting into anger. An anger he directed at the woman who had ended Rosie's life and taken Lucy away from him all over again—the woman who had dared to penetrate the part of him that was so carefully sealed away.

"I am so, so sorry," she repeated.

Jake towered above her, fists tightly clenched as rage seeped from his every pore. His voice was icy cold. "You did this?"

Cass tried to explain, stumbling on the words. "The pony was suffering. I had no other option."

He just stared at her, taut-jawed and hollow-eyed. "Donald could have saved her. Why isn't he here?"

"No one could have saved her. It was too late."

Jake's face was blank, expressionless. "I want a postmortem."

Her heart thudded hard inside her chest as she fought for breath "I'll do it right now."

"No!" He turned on his heel. "I'll get Donald to do it."

She watched his tall, angular figure disappear across the yard, back toward the stable, not realizing she was twisting her fingers fiercely together until she felt the warmth of a rough hand over hers.

"I am so sorry, lass," Bill Munro said with a sad smile. "I know you had to do it. I can only apologize for my son but he does have his reasons for being so hostile."

"I am truly sorry about your pony," she said again, pushing her hands deep into her pockets. "Are you sure you don't want me to do a postmortem right now?"

Bill shook his head. "Thanks, but we'd better leave it to Donald.... No doubt Jake will be apologizing after."

"I don't need his apologies," she said quietly, walking to her car. "I did what I had to do...as he'll find out."

CHAPTER TWO

Cass drove back to the clinic on autopilot, her heart heavy with a dull ache that spread through her whole body. She'd had no choice, she knew that, and so did the old man who'd given his permission. Healing the pain of innocent animals was the whole reason she'd become a vet. The taking of life was the dark side of her job, but sometimes necessary. It had been a sad relief to see the pain-misted eyes of the sweet little pony glaze over. Surely the man…Jake… must have understood that. Then why had he been so hostile? Or was that just his way of dealing with pain?

The older man, Bill, had followed Cass to her car, still trying to explain. Rosie had been Jake's daughter's pony, he said, his last real link with her, so obviously he was upset. Normally, the only vet Jake ever allowed near his horses was Donald, which didn't help the situation.

What had happened to his daughter? Cass wondered, looking out for the sign to Little Dale. She would be glad when today was over and she could forget about Jake Munro and the poor, unfortunate pony— not that there was much chance of that, she realized. The memories were already crowding back. What was it about the man that had made such an impression on her, anyway?

She would never forget the echoing ring of horse's hooves on the hard surface of the yard, breaking the awful silence of death in the barn and giving her an excuse to escape from the emotion that threatened to suffocate her. She had stepped out into the dusk of evening in a daze, blinking to focus in the half light as Jake Munro appeared from the shadows, looming above her. For some reason, it was his scuffed tan boots that she'd noticed first. Her gaze had settled on their well-worn toes, traveling up jean-clad legs to finally meet his glittering blue eyes, eyes that had held hers with such a fierce intensity it seemed for a moment as if the world stood still. And for one crazy, endless second she had wanted to run into his arms and release all the agony of the last half hour.

Cass blinked hard, focusing on her driving—anything to cut out the embarrassment of that moment. Was she going absolutely crazy, reacting like that to a total stranger?

"Cass Truman," she told herself out loud. "You need to get a grip. It wasn't the first time you've had a hard task, and it sure won't be the last, so get over it."

The sign for the clinic loomed ahead. With a sigh of relief, she pulled into the cobbled yard behind the huddle of buildings and cut the engine, allowing her thoughts to go back to the poor old pony once again. Damn Jake Munro. She'd done what she had to do, she knew that, and if he demanded a postmortem, then he would know it, too.

"BIT OF TROUBLE TODAY, Cassandra?"

Todd Andrews, her boss at Low Fell Animal Clinic, looked up with a quizzical smile as Cass walked in. Despite his pleasant expression, she could see that he wasn't happy. Her heart sank. She was still on probation here, and she could do without upsetting the boss on her first day.

"Not really. Nothing I couldn't handle," she answered in a matter-of-fact tone. "It had to be done, and if the pony's owner was upset, I apologize. I'm here to care for animals, though, not people."

"Whoa...pony? I was talking about Tom Alston."

An image of the angry, muddy farmer flashed back into her mind and she rolled her eyes, shrugging. "He doesn't like new vets, that's all. Especially slightly-built female ones, I guess, as he kept harping on about me not being strong enough to do the job. Well, I am strong enough, and I can't do anything about my gender, can I?"

Suddenly Todd grinned, his expression relaxing. "Look Cassandra," he began.

"Cass," she cut in. "Sorry, I hate Cassandra."

Todd ignored her comment. "You're bound to have the occasional problem with the older farmers around here, I'm afraid. Some of them are still living in the 1960s. Could you just try and charm them a little? It might help."

"I'm not that good on charm," Cass replied. "But I will try. Men like Tom Alston drive me nuts, though."

"He's just a struggling hill farmer, like a lot of others around here." Todd sighed, running one hand through his curly gray hair. "He's trying to make a living in the same way as his father and his grandfather did before him when it's hardly possible anymore."

Cass's face softened. "I guess," she agreed. "It's just that I hate being bullied."

"So what was the problem with the pony then?" Todd asked reluctantly. The phone rang before Cass could complete her explanation. Todd held the phone away from his ear and Jake's raised voice boomed out into the room.

"How could she have been so sure it was a twisted gut? She should've called for backup...rung you...anything!"

Todd's thick, dark eyebrows drew together, meeting in an arc above his nose. Cass found herself concentrating on them as she listened to her boss's calm, deep voice assuring Jake that she was well qualified and promising a postmortem first thing in the morning.

Todd hung up and sighed again. "He wants Donald to do the postmortem."

"I don't care what Jake Munro says," she snapped. "Or what his excuses are. The pony was suffering—his father could see it. He agreed with me. I could have done the postmortem there and then, shown him the proof. I offered."

"He will only have Donald," Todd repeated. "He's our best horse vet, after all."

Hot color flooded Cass's face. "I'm really sorry for going on about this, but I know I did the right thing. I suppose the whole situation upset me, to be honest. The pony was so sweet." She held up her hands, smiling apologetically. "I know that's not very professional."

"There's nothing wrong with caring," Todd said.

"Well, do you think I could at least go along with Donald tomorrow? I'd really like to see this through."

She twisted her fingers together, wondering if now was the right time to tell her new boss about her ambitions for the future.

"I really want to specialize in horses, as well, and it would be good experience."

Todd smiled, placing a hand on her shoulder. "I'm glad to hear that. I like to encourage ambition in my staff. It will have to be very early tomorrow, though. He has to be in Doncaster by afternoon."

"Thanks." Cass removed bottles of medication from her bag, putting them carefully back into the refrigerator. "And I'm sorry for upsetting your clients."

"Oh, they'll get used to you eventually," Todd said.

CASS SLICED CHEESE on a piece of bread and doubled it into a sandwich. But after the events of the day, she couldn't even think about cooking—or eating—at all, she decided, placing it back on the plate.

A vivid memory of the sweet little pony filled her mind and sadness welled up inside her. There was nothing more she could have done, however, and tomorrow would prove it.

Flipping open her phone case, she pressed Home on her contacts list. The ringing droned in her ears and she canceled the call, scrolling down to her dad's cell number. When she heard his familiar voice, warm and vibrant, tears pressed against her eyelids.

"Hi, Dad, it's just me. How's Mum?"

Her jovial tone sounded forced, and he obviously knew it.

"You really don't need to worry, Cass. It was just a scare, a false alarm. She wouldn't even have told you at all if I hadn't insisted."

"I'm not a kid anymore, Dad. I need to know these things. She should have told me right away."

"That's what I said, love. Anyway, how are you, and how's that new job of yours going?"

By the time Cass had related her experience at Sky View to her dad and made him chuckle at her story about the manure-splattered farmer, she felt a whole lot better.

"Now don't you worry about us," her dad told her. "Just concentrate on your career. We might come over to see you soon, if we can get anyone to mind the store for a day or two."

Feeling calmer after talking to her dad,

Cass finished her light meal and called it a night, expecting to find sleep elusive. However, her eyes closed as soon as her head hit the pillow, and the next thing she knew, the school bell was ringing in her dreams, calling her in to lessons. She jerked awake, reaching out to turn off her alarm clock, totally in the present as the events of yesterday came back to her.

The sun was hardly over the hills when Cass and Donald set off for Sky View Stables.

The middle-aged vet glanced across at her. "You're very quiet," he remarked, nosing his large four-by-four up the narrow lane.

Cass might have been sitting beside him but her head was definitely elsewhere.

He tried again. "You okay, lass? Don't let Jake upset you."

Cass started, her thoughts rushing back to the present. "Oh, I'm not letting him upset me. I was just miles away."

"I could see that. In a nice place, I hope."

"I've always been a bit of a dreamer, I'm afraid—one of my worse traits. To be honest, I was thinking about my mum. She hasn't been well."

"I'm sorry to hear that."

Noting the kind expression on his face, she felt a flush creep up her cheeks. "Thanks. And…look, I'm really sorry about you having to do this postmortem. I could easily have done it myself yesterday."

"No worries," Donald said. "I think I need to apologize on Jake's behalf. He can be a bit touchy, but he does have his reasons."

"That's exactly what Todd said," Cass murmured. "But surely there's no excuse for downright rudeness?"

Donald smiled. "I heard that Tom Alston was pretty rude to you yesterday, too, but that doesn't seem to have got to you."

Cass twisted around to face him, her interest raised. "What is this reason, for Jake Munro's attitude? Or is it just an excuse?"

Donald put the vehicle into gear. It juddered violently, throwing Cass into the window.

"Hey," she cried. "I do want to get there, you know."

"Sorry, this old vehicle could do with

some attention. Anyway, are you sure about that, after yesterday…getting there, I mean?"

Cass's mouth set into a firm line as she glanced at him, catching his eye.

"Yesterday would have been a tragedy no matter who owned the little mare. I did what needed to be done. There's no doubt in my mind about that."

"Good for you." He nodded. "And I guess you'll be looking forward to saying 'I told you so.' Is that why you wanted to come?"

Cass's response was immediate. "No, not at all. I came because I want to see it through. The guy was obviously very upset. Anyone would be. It still doesn't give him the right to be so unpleasant."

"What if I told you that his mother and little daughter were both killed in an accident a while ago," Donald said quietly, concentrating on the road ahead. "And he doesn't like people to talk about it, so you never heard it from me."

A lurch of sympathy left Cass momentarily speechless. "I didn't realize," she eventually managed. "And of course the chestnut was his daughter's pony."

Donald shrugged. "Yes, but you weren't to know. It wouldn't have made any difference, anyway…if she did have a twisted gut."

Cass fought back a sharp retort, staring out the window but seeing nothing. Jake would understand soon enough, and then maybe next time no one would question her.

"Was it his fault?" she asked quietly.

"Oh, no," Donald said. "Well, at least not directly. I think he may blame himself, though. He was away, competing in Europe, when it happened."

"Competing?" echoed Cass.

Donald nodded, carefully negotiating the entrance to Sky View.

"He used to show jump. Top level, too. He gave it up after the accident."

"So what does he do now?"

Cass's question fell on deaf ears as Jake Munro's tall figure materialized in front of the Land Rover, forcing it to stop. He was just as she remembered—ruggedly handsome and fierce, his expression extremely arrogant. Was he like that before the accident? Somehow, Cass thought he probably was.

The tense line of his jaw softened when Donald climbed out of the vehicle. Jake almost smiled.

"Morning," he called, holding out his hand and ignoring Cass. Donald took it, pumping it up and down, his soft white fingers clutched in Jake's broad, suntanned grip.

"Bad business," Donald remarked. "How are you holding up?"

Jake's response was curt and to the point. "These things happen. I just needed to be sure."

He looked pointedly at Cass, who held his gaze unflinchingly, raising her chin with an air of defiance.

"I'm already sure," she said.

"Right, then," interrupted Donald. "Let's get on with it."

Jake watched, arms wrapped across his chest and dark eyes narrowed, until Donald took out his scalpel. Then he turned on his heel and walked away to lean against the paddock fence, resting his head on his forearms. For a moment, Cass felt like going to him and placing her hand on his taut shoulders. No matter how irritating he was, the poor guy was suffering—she could see that.

"Look at this," Donald said, getting her attention.

Cass had seen enough postmortems and dead creatures in the last few years to make her pretty hardened. They'd gone to a better place—it was only their owners who suffered now. But this pony, Rosie, had gotten to her somehow. She was glad of the blanket someone had so thoughtfully laid over her, relieved not to see her glazed eyes.

Donald was on his knees.

"Look," he repeated. "Half the gut must have already been dead when you euthanized her. Poor little beggar."

A shadow fell across them, and Cass glanced up to see Jake. His face was expressionless.

"Good job Cass acted quickly, as far as I can see," Donald said. "I'll tidy up here while you go and put the kettle on."

"I'll finish for you if you like," Cass offered.

"Is that it then?" Jake said, his voice cracking. He cleared his throat, turning away abruptly.

"Thanks, Cass," Donald cut in before she could respond, obviously trying to lighten the mood. He stood up, smiling. "I think I'll take you on all my jobs." When they both ignored him, he walked off toward the house. "I guess I'll go put the kettle on myself, then," he called.

Jake began to follow him, but stopped to look back at Cass, holding her defiant gaze.

"I really am sorry about Rosie," she said quietly, her expression softening. "It must be tough for you."

"What, no 'I told you so?'" he retorted.

She just shook her head, turning her attention back to the job at hand, and he glared at her for another moment before striding off after Donald.

"No change there, then," she murmured. Cass finished up and put Donald's bag back in the Land Rover before following the two men across the yard toward the square, stone cottage. It should have been a pretty building, she thought, but the roses that had once grown around the front door looked half-dead, and the whole place needed fresh paint and some TLC. She found herself wondering what it had been like when Jake's mother was alive.

A man's deep voice interrupted her daydream.

"They'll be round the back in the kitchen."

Looking up with a start, she saw Bill Munro standing in the shadow of an oak tree at the side of the yard, one hand stroking his bearded chin.

She smiled impulsively, pleased to see the old man. He fell into step beside her.

"You were right, then?" he asked.

"You knew I was."

He nodded slowly.

"Yes, I knew, but there's no telling Jake. He had to see for himself."

"I don't suppose I'll get an apology."

Bill's bright blue eyes sparkled. "You've already sussed him out, I see."

Cass wanted to tell Bill how sorry she was to hear about his wife and granddaughter, but it wasn't her business, and she didn't want him to think she'd been prying.

Bill walked with her toward the kitchen door. "Staying around here long?" he asked.

Cass shrugged, smiling. "I hope to. I like the beautiful wild countryside and the tranquility."

"You're staying at the B and B, I believe?"

She glanced at him in amusement.

"Does everyone know everything around here? It's temporary, while I look for somewhere to rent."

"What, you mean a cottage or something?"

"Something," she responded. "I'm not really sure, to be honest. I could do with a place for six months or so. I'm only on a six-month contract at the moment—a kind of trial period, I suppose you'd call it."

She placed her hand on the dull brass handle in front of her, pressing it down with a sense of foreboding. The door was scratched and dirty, and desperate for a coat of paint. She looked over at Bill.

"Are you coming in?"

He turned away, shaking his head.

"Better things to do. I'll no doubt see you soon."

"No doubt," she agreed.

As Cass pushed open the door, a heavy sadness weighed her down. There was an emptiness to this place, a total lack—or loss—of love. She had a definite feeling that Jake and his dad spent most of their time avoiding each other and found herself wondering what Sky View had been like when Jake's mother and daughter were around.

Entering the kitchen, Cass saw the two men at once. They were deep in conversation, their heads lowered as they studied something on the table. She stepped inside, taking in her surroundings. The room was large and bright with sunshine, a lovely, homey place despite the clutter that crowded every available surface.

"Hi," she called awkwardly.

Donald glanced up, smiling. "We're just looking at stud books. There's coffee in the pot. Help yourself."

Cass poured a mug and added milk, sipping it slowly without looking at Jake. "So…" she said. "I guess you're a breeder."

Jake ignored her, but Donald filled the gap. "Only a couple of foals a year at the moment, but he buys and sells a lot of young stock. Don't you, Jake?"

Forced to join in the conversation, Jake met her gaze. His eyes were like his dad's, but without the sparkle. "Just trying to make a living," he said.

The sound of Donald's chair scraping across the floor as he stood up broke the ensuing silence. He reached for his jacket, slinging it over his shoulder. "Come on then, Cass," he told her. "I don't mean to make you rush your drink, but I'm supposed to be in Doncaster by early afternoon. I'll see you soon, Jake, hopefully in better circumstances."

"Is he always so antisocial?" Cass asked as she and Donald clambered into his four-by-four.

Donald concentrated on the narrow lane ahead of them, slowing down and pressing on his horn to chase away a small, black-headed rough fell sheep. It stood in the road and stared at the vehicle with yellow-ringed eyes.

"You'd think they owned the road," he declared as it sauntered off.

"I guess they do around here," Cass remarked thoughtfully. "Was it long ago, the accident that killed Jake Munro's family?"

"About twelve months, almost to the day. Lucy was a lovely little girl, only five years old. Her gran, Gwen, was one of those salt-of-the-earth people who would do anything to help anyone. Such a tragedy. He has a son, too—Lucy's twin, Robbie. He went to live with his mother after the funeral. The whole business totally destroyed Jake. He gave up competing altogether, but he's still a top-class trainer, specializing in problem horses." A wry grin flashed across his face. "I think it's the horses that keep him going, but as you already know, he doesn't have much time for people."

"You can say that again. He doesn't even seem to have time for his dad."

Donald frowned. "I don't think either of them has half begun to get over their loss. He's a great guy, Bill. He used to be in on all the local action, you know, committees and things. He raised a lot of money for charity a couple of years ago. Now I guess he's just kind of empty."

"It takes a long time to get over a tragedy like that," Cass said. "If you ever really do, that is."

Donald pulled over outside the vet clinic, leaving his engine running. "Oh, Bill will get there," he insisted. "Jake, now, I'm not so sure about. Anyway, thanks for your company, but out you get. I'm late as it is. You'll have to come and have dinner with us one night. Meet the brood. I'll get Jenny to give you a call."

Cass got out of the vehicle, glancing back inside before she slammed the door. "Thanks, Donald," she said. "I'd like that."

Somehow it felt as if she'd just made a friend.

CHAPTER THREE

TODD WAS IN the surgery going through some paperwork. He looked up when he heard Cass come into the room, peering impatiently at her over his glasses.

"How did it go?"

She shrugged. "I knew how it would go. The poor little pony was in a bad state."

He went back to his work, leaning forward over the desk.

"Well, that's good then. Oh, and Mary Park is in the waiting room. Would you mind having a look at her dog? She doesn't have an appointment but she's a bit upset, says someone ran him over."

"Of course," Cass said, pulling on a white coat and pushing open the door into Reception.

The woman sat on a chair that was too small for her large frame. A bright-eyed Yorkshire terrier she clutched wriggled in her arms.

"Mrs. Park, is it?" Cass asked with her best professional smile, pushing all thoughts of Jake Munro and his tragedy out of her head. "What can I do for you?"

"Mary," she said, struggling to her feet. "Call me Mary. It's Poppy here. He ran into the road in front of a car..."

"Well let's go into the examining room and I'll check him out," Cass suggested, already leading the way.

After a thorough examination of Poppy, Cass looked up at his worried owner with a broad grin.

"Well, Mary, you'll be pleased to know there's absolutely nothing to worry about. He has a scuff on his shoulder, that's all, and he may be feeling a bit bruised."

The woman's round, pleasant face contorted into an expression of pained relief. "But are you sure?"

Cass picked up the little dog, settling him in his mistress's outstretched arms.

"One hundred per cent. Now don't let him run out into the road again. He might not be so lucky next time."

Todd appeared just as they were leaving the examining room.

"I'm glad that Poppy seems to be okay," he said.

"You've taken on a good vet this time Todd," Mary told him. "She's sorted my Poppy out good and proper."

"Glad to hear it." He held the front door to let her out.

"There wasn't actually anything wrong with him," Cass admitted as it shut behind them.

Todd grinned. "You'll soon get to know Poppy—he's one of our most regular visitors. Oh, and…" He paused. "I know you aren't really supposed to be on surgery, but I'm afraid I have to pop out, so would you mind? There's a bit of a line building up, I'm afraid."

BY LUNCHTIME CASS had seen two cats with fur balls and one with a ripped ear, an elderly, bedraggled hamster, five more dogs and a parrot that was pulling out its feathers.

I can really identify with that parrot, she thought as she started to tidy up. Suddenly a sit-down and a coffee seemed very appealing. She was about ready to leave when Sally, the receptionist, popped her head around the door.

"You have a visitor," she said. "And he doesn't seem to have a pet."

Cass frowned. Whoever would be visiting her at the clinic? She didn't even know anyone around here yet.

Sally hesitated.

"I'll send him in, shall I?"

"He?" Cass echoed as Sally's perfectly made-up face disappeared again. Could it be Jake Munro coming to apologize, perhaps? Fat chance of that. Cass's mind wandered back to the moment when she first saw him, and something tightened in her throat. He had seemed... What, she asked herself, what had he seemed?

"We meet again," said a familiar voice, and Cass looked up in surprise to meet... not quite the icy blue eyes that kept haunting her thoughts, but something very similar.

"Bill," her visitor announced, holding out his hand. "Munro. Remember, from Sky View," he added, as she stood with her mouth open.

"Of course." She placed her hand in his

calloused palm. "How could I ever forget? What can I do for you?"

"Well, it's really more what I can do for you."

"For me?"

He nodded. "Yes… You said you needed somewhere to rent, and I have a vacant cottage. It's small, but it's a pretty little place and quite enough space for one." His bushy gray brows drew together. "I take it there is only one?"

Cass laughed. "Oh, yes, just me, I'm afraid. I have enough trouble trying to sort myself out."

"So what do you say? I was about to put it in the hands of a rental agency, but if you need somewhere…"

"Well, I do, but what about your son? He and I didn't get off to the best start. I don't think he would appreciate me living nearby."

"Jake?" snorted Bill. "It has nothing to do with him. The cottages are how I make my income, and I'll rent them to whoever I like. Anyway…" His face creased in a smile. "It's not as if it's right on the doorstep of Sky View. More like just around the corner."

Cass felt happiness bubbling up inside. She belonged somewhere at last. "Well, then, I would love to come and see it," she said. "After work today, perhaps? I don't have a shift tonight, and for once I'm not even on call."

"Any time is okay by me," Bill said. "Say around seven?"

"See you at seven," she agreed. "Just tell me where to go."

IT WAS A BRIGHT, sunlit evening, the kind where the whole world seems abuzz with joy. Cass felt some of that joy as she drove toward Sky View. She had a good job, a job she could really come to love, and now she might even have a new home. Not a shared flat, but her very own place, here in some of the most beautiful countryside she'd ever seen.

The wind blew in through her open window and she breathed in the country scents as she left the village, humming softly to the strains of a modern love song. Love! It was totally overrated as far as she was concerned. Her fellow students had been constantly falling in and out of love, one minute wandering around with their heads in a euphoric cloud and in the next, totally inconsolable.

Sometimes Cass worried that there was something wrong with her because she'd never really fallen for anyone. There had been boyfriends, of course, but they'd been kind of lukewarm relationships, more friendships than love affairs. Her mind wandered back to the day Jamie had told her it was over. She had been seeing him for almost six months, but when he finally plucked up the courage to tell her he had met someone else, all she'd felt was a sense of relief.

Her only real passion had been the same since she was twelve years old—the passion to become a vet that had arisen on the day Bud died in her arms. Everything else had taken second place since that day, as if she'd been driven by the desire to make amends for her lack of knowledge.... And now that she'd fulfilled her goal, now that she had the opportunity to stop and reflect, love and romance still didn't figure in her scheme of things.

Her parents had lived to work, with little time to spare for their child. Cass felt she had inherited that drive from them, as if her ambition overrode everything else. She couldn't picture herself having the time to give a husband and children the attention they needed. She'd once thought that when she was finally qualified as a vet, she'd be able to slow down and start a family. But now that she'd finished school and begun her career, she wanted to push herself further. Beyond honing her skills, she wanted to specialize in equestrian medicine and become highly respected for her expertise. Did that make her selfish? she wondered. Surely it would be worse to have a family and neglect them.

As she carefully negotiated the narrow lane that ran across the steep Lakeland fell side on a wonderful summer's evening, those early years at college seemed so very long ago. All the nights spent in a tiny, basically furnished room, poring over books and files and forgetting to eat while her flatmates went out partying. They told her she was crazy, but she didn't care. In fact, if it hadn't been for her mother packing up a huge box of groceries for her on the rare occasions when she went home to visit, Cass reckoned she might just have wasted away.

Turning away from the past, Cass peered over the steering wheel, looking for the sign to Sky View. Bill Munro had told her to take a sharp right down a narrow grassy track once she'd gone through the gate. She nosed her car along the path, then rounded a corner to see a pretty little stone cottage. Her heart raced. Could this really be it?

Bill appeared just as she switched off the engine. He raised one hand in welcome while fumbling in his pocket with the other, withdrawing a set of keys.

"Hi," she called, falling into step beside him, trying to look calm but struggling to control her excitement.

He flashed her a smile. "It's very small, you know."

"It's so pretty," she exclaimed as the front door swung open.

"And there is no central heating, just old-fashioned electric heaters," he warned.

Cass locked her fingers together. "Is there a fire?"

"Better than that," Bill declared. "There's a wood-burning stove and a good stack of dry logs in the shed around the back."

As a vision of herself basking in the warm glow of burning logs after a hard day at work slid into her mind's eye, a smile spread across Cass's face. "I'll take it," she said.

"But you haven't seen everything yet," Bill reminded her. "And you don't even know how much I'm going to charge."

Cass flushed, feeling stupid. It wasn't like her to be so impulsive.

"Let's have a proper look around, and then we can talk business," Bill suggested. "Of course, you might find it a bit too isolated. It can be pretty bleak here in the winter."

"Nowhere is too isolated for me," Cass said, welcoming the idea. "And anyway… I might get a dog for company."

The vague idea, now put into words, made her feel panicky. What was she talking about? Having her own dog had been a plan for the future—somewhere in her dreams. Did she really even want a dog? Was she ready for that kind of commitment?

Oblivious to her doubts, Bill nodded. "That's a good idea. In fact, we have some pups for sale at the farm, you'll have to come and see them."

As soon as the words left Bill's lips, he realized it was a bad idea. Technically, they were Jake's pups, and it was pretty obvious that his son had taken a real dislike to his prospective tenant— mainly because of Rosie, of course, but it was more than that. After Tara let him down so badly, he seemed to avoid all contact with women. Cass was nothing like Tara, although… Bill cast her a sidelong glance. She might not have had Jake's ex-wife's glamorous good looks, but the young vet certainly did have something. An innocent, untouched beauty.

Suddenly, Bill found himself questioning his decision to offer her the cottage at all. He and Jake had drifted apart since the accident.… He took a breath. He and his son needed to build bridges, and bringing Cass here might be knocking them down.

"You would probably be happier closer to the village, don't you think?" he asked. "Closer to work and…"

His voice trailed off as he noted the disappointment in her dark eyes. "You've changed your mind, haven't you?" she said sadly.

"No, of course not. It's just…"

"You don't need to worry," she assured him. "I won't come anywhere near the farm, and I'll stay well away from your son, if that's what this is about. He won't even know I'm here."

"Well, in that case…" Bill held out his hand. "It's five hundred a month, payment in advance, and you pay the council tax and any fuel bills."

Cass took his hand and shook it firmly for the second time that day. "It's a deal. I'll move my stuff in tomorrow, if that's okay."

"Whenever you like." The older man smiled. Never mind what Jake thought, he decided. She seemed like a lovely young woman, and maybe Jake would eventually discover that for himself.

THE IDEA OF having a dog had sprung itself on Cass. It wasn't until she'd announced her intention to Bill that she realized it had been preying on her mind. She hadn't even thought about owning another dog since Bud, but maybe she had finally come full circle.

She drove slowly back toward Little Dale, allowing her mind to wander back to the day her little ginger terrier cross had run out in front of a car. Bud had been a present from her parents on her ninth birthday and her constant companion from the day he arrived until that terrible day in the lane that changed her whole focus on life. Even now, a lump caught in her throat as she imagined his bright face. With her parents constantly busy in the shop and no siblings, she had spent hours with Bud in the fields around their village. Losing him had left a huge shadow over her life, especially when she found out that she could probably have saved him if she'd known how to staunch the bleeding. That was the day she decided to become a vet, and she had never swayed from her purpose.

Feeling the sudden weight of sadness,

Cass pulled over and cut the engine, looking down into the valley far below without, for once, taking in the beauty of the scene. The memory of Bud's trusting little face broke her heart. Did she really want a dog again, after all this time?

The sound of hooves brought her out of her reverie as they clip-clopped hollowly along the lane behind her. Twisting around in her seat, she saw a horse and rider trotting toward her. A big gray, its hatless rider sitting tall. Jake Munro! He was the last person she wanted to see, but it was too late to start her engine and pull out. The hoof beats grew closer and she leaned down to fumble in her bag, trying to look busy while wondering why she should care if he saw her sitting idly by the side of the road.

"Having trouble?"

His voice was just as she remembered, deep and melodic. Why did she feel like such an idiot?

She glanced up, not quite meeting his eyes, cursing the blush she could feel spreading on her face. "No, thanks. Just looking for something."

"I saw you driving out of Sky View."

Jutting out her chin, she regained her confidence. "Yes," she said, determined not to be daunted by his sheer masculinity. "I've just rented a cottage from your dad."

The icy glint in his blue eyes could have pierced her soul, but she held his gaze without faltering.

"Don't worry, though—it's quite far from the farm, so you won't have to see me."

He swung his mount away.

"It makes no difference to me where you live."

The angry set of his jaw belied his pronouncement, and Cass found herself hoping he wouldn't give poor Bill a hard time.

"Look," she called after him. "I needed somewhere to stay, and your dad had the perfect place going begging."

Jake reined in, turning his prancing horse back to face her. The wild-eyed gray mare tossed her beautiful head and foam flew like snowflakes.

"I already told you," he repeated drily. "It means nothing to me where you live."

"If this is still about Rosie, then I'm sorry, but you know it had to be done."

Across the short distance, she could see the pain flashing across his face. "I just like my own space, that's all."

He hesitated then, as if searching for the right words.

"And…and I do know you did the pony a favor."

As he rode away, Cass couldn't help watching. Man and horse moved as one. She felt a rush of empathy. He, too, understood the joy of the companionship with animals and appreciated their uncomplicated affection.

CHAPTER FOUR

CARLOTTA SIDLED, OBVIOUSLY disturbed by her rider's mood. After four years, the mare was used to Jake's ways—today the tension in him must have buzzed like an electric current. She moved out into the road, prancing sideways and snorting, taking his attention for a moment. His firm hand on the reins calmed her at once.

"Okay, easy, girl."

However angry he felt inside—and he felt angry, foolish even, about the fact that his father had gone behind his back like that—he tried to make a point of never allowing it to spill over into his riding. Just being on a horse usually took his mind off everything life seemed determined to throw at him, but the woman had managed to play havoc with that simple rule. Anyway, it shouldn't have been *her* telling him that she'd rented the cottage, it should have been his dad. And for that matter, it would have been nice to have been consulted in the first place. A hollow laugh eased his tension. Since when had his father ever consulted him about anything?

A vehicle approached from behind, and Jake ran his hand down Carlotta's arched neck. There was no way he was going to let a vehicle squeeze past on this narrow stretch of road. It would just have to wait. Moving into a jog trot he glanced back, noting the green hatchback following them...*her* hatchback. Had she been sent here solely to annoy him? With another brief look at the pale face over the steering wheel, he turned Carlotta onto the grass verge, dug in his heels and urged her into a canter. Only too happy to oblige, the mare bunched up her quarters, sank into her hocks and sprang, clearing the wall at the side of the lane as if it was nothing and landing with an ecstatic buck.

A sudden rush of adrenaline released his mind, if only momentarily, from the pain of reality. Jake turned back, raising a hand toward the woman before heading off at a gallop. The look of amazement on her face brought a sense of satisfaction, and he leaned forward, absorbing the sheer elation of the power beneath him.

Horses had long been his escape when things went wrong. He had used the challenge and excitement of competition to try to get his life back on track after Tara's defection, but riding hadn't been nearly enough to fill the void left by Lucy and his mum. Reining in, Jake stared down into the valley, watching the green vehicle snaking its way down to the village. Nothing could ever fill that gaping hole in his life, or assuage the guilt and pain that constantly clawed at his gut.

Slowly, he turned Carlotta homeward. When she dutifully obeyed, moving quietly across the steep hillside, he closed his eyes for a moment, trying to stifle the sob that rose inside him.

CASS DROVE SLOWLY back to the village. After hearing about Jake Munro's loss, she wouldn't have been human if she hadn't felt some sympathy for him. His attitude, however, did him no favors. Many people lost loved ones without taking their bitterness out on the whole world. And what was that crazy jump all about? It was foolhardy, to say the least. Perhaps losing his family had sent Jake over the edge. And what about Lucy's mother? No one ever mentioned her. Did Jake have a wife tucked away somewhere perhaps?

Jake Munro was still invading Cass's thoughts as she pulled in outside the B and B and cut her engine. There was no denying his skill with horses—he and the high-strung gray mare had seemed to move as one entity. Pity he didn't have the same connection with humans.

Grabbing her bag from the back of the car, she ran up the steps to the square white guesthouse where she'd been staying since arriving in Little Dale. She had discovered it when she came for her interview at Low Fell Animal Clinic a couple of weeks earlier. The owner, Clare Biggins, had made her so welcome that Cass had booked in there as soon as she heard the job was hers. It was only fair to let Clare know as soon as possible that she was leaving tomorrow. She would pay her until the end of the week, but she couldn't wait that long to move in to the cottage. Her own place, at last, and the start of a brand-new life.

To CASS'S RELIEF, Clare was almost as excited as she was about the cottage. "I know Sky Cottage," she exclaimed, her round face shining with genuine delight. "Even its name is magical, and it's so pretty, like something out of a storybook. Won't you be a bit nervous, though, living in the middle of nowhere on your own...not to mention lonely?"

"It's not that far from Sky View," Cass reminded her. "Only a few minutes' walk. And I'm going to get a dog for company."

"A dog!" Clare said. "Are you sure they allow dogs, though? Lots of rented places have a strictly no-pets policy."

Cass's face fell. She hadn't thought about that. "I did say something about it to Bill Munro, and he never said anything. He even told me his son has some puppies for sale."

"Well, there you go, then." Clare smiled. "Obviously they don't mind dogs."

"I think Jake Munro would *mind* just

about anything to do with me. We didn't get off on a very good footing, I'm afraid."

Clare shrugged. "He doesn't seem to be in a very good place with anyone," she said sadly. "It was bad enough that his wife left him, but losing Lucy and Gwen must have been too much to bear."

Cass felt her irritation at Jake's behavior fading. "He had a wife? I wondered what happened to Lucy's mother."

"I don't really like to gossip," Clare replied awkwardly. "He was living down south at the time, anyway, so no one from around here really knew anything about his wife—except that she went off to follow a singing career, leaving the twins behind with their dad. That was when he came back to Sky View. Gwen, his mum, was a lovely lady, and she was happy to help look after the children. I don't know how he and Bill have been coping since the accident…"

"I guess it's just a case of having to," Cass suggested thoughtfully. "Donald mentioned something about Robbie going to live with his mum. Was he Lucy's twin?"

Clare nodded. "She took him away with her after the funeral. I don't know whether it was her idea or Jake's. But tell me some more about the cottage. Exactly when are you moving in?"

Cass frowned, her thoughts still on the tragedy that must have turned Jake and Bill's whole world upside down. Bud's death had changed her life, and sad though it was, a pet's death couldn't even come close to losing a wife, a daughter and a mum. An image of Jake's bleak, angry face slid into her mind. Did he ever smile? she wondered. What was he like before the accident? Perhaps he should have kept Robbie with him—having the little boy to care for might have helped him to move on and find something to smile about again.

Clare touched her arm. "So…when are you leaving us?"

"Sorry," Cass apologized. "I was miles away. I'm moving in tomorrow, but I'll pay you for the whole week."

"You don't have to do that. I'll miss the company, of course, and the money, but I really am happy for you. I just hope you don't get too lonely out there by yourself."

"But I won't be alone, will I?" Cass laughed. "I'll have a dog to keep me company."

JAKE LEAPED EASILY down from the saddle, ran his stirrup irons up the leather and gave Carlotta an affectionate pat.

"What would I do without you, girl?" he asked, pulling the reins over her ears to lead her across the yard to her stable. The gray mare nodded, as if in understanding, and followed obediently.

Jake's eyes were drawn to the space in the yard where poor Rosie had lain, awaiting collection. A sigh of relief passed his lips, accompanied by a lurch of guilt at not being there when they came for her. His dad would probably say he had run away from his responsibilities, just as he always did, but it wasn't true. Rosie was gone, and there was nothing more he could have done for her. When Tara left he had run away, throwing himself into his career instead of staying home and taking care of Lucy and Robbie. He knew that only too well now, and he would be paying for it for the rest of his life. A sharp pain tore at his stomach, bringing a rush of bile into his mouth. He didn't deserve to feel any happiness when little Lucy and his mum were no longer here to feel anything at all, and Robbie was gone to the other side of the world.

Oh, how he hoped his son was okay. A few minutes on the phone once a week, if he was lucky, told him nothing, and the darned lawyer he'd hired to try and get Robbie back was worse than useless. The memory of Tara's bitter voice in his ears, when he eventually managed to get hold of her after the funeral, doubled the heavy burden of guilt he felt every single day of his life.

You aren't fit to be a father. Robbie is staying in America with me now. I know I went away, but I thought I was doing the best thing for them by leaving them with their dad. You're the one who really abandoned them.

The accusation rang inside Jake's head. Was she right? Had he abandoned them? The answer came at once. Yes, in a way he had, running around Europe, throwing himself into the thrill of competition when his kids needed him. His poor, dear mother had never once complained about his being away so often. Perhaps she should have. She would still be here if he'd faced up to his responsibilities for once. A sob rose in his throat and he forced it back, turning his attention to the gray mare standing patiently beside him.

BILL MUNRO SAW his son clatter into the yard and vault down from Carlotta, saw the expression on Jake's face as he gave the mare an affectionate stroke. It seemed that Jake could only really communicate with animals nowadays. Setting his jaw, the old man headed purposefully toward him. Gwen would have told them both to get on with their lives, but it was just so hard. But he owed it to her to at least try to get Jake's life back on track.

"Good ride, son?" he asked.

Jake glanced sideways at him. "They turned up for her, then."

Bill nodded. "Yes, about two."

"I'm sorry." He turned away, unable to meet his father's eyes. "I should have seen to it myself."

"No, really. It isn't a problem.... Sad, though."

Jake's eyes darkened. "It should never have happened."

"There are a lot of things around here that shouldn't have happened," Bill agreed. Tentatively he placed a hand on his son's shoulder. "They say it gets easier with time."

Jake shrugged off his sympathy. "It will never get easier," he declared, leading Carlotta into her stall.

Bill shook his gray head sadly. "We have to try and get on with our lives, son. I know the anniversary has made it all raw again, but somehow we have to get through it."

"Why did you rent Sky Cottage to that girl?"

Jake's unexpected question took Bill totally by surprise. It held an accusation that brought out a sudden prickle of anger in him.

"I'll rent the cottage to whoever I please. She's in a strange place with a new job and she needed somewhere to live. And she's hardly a girl. She must be almost as old as you are."

"She doesn't look it," Jake responded. "She's hardly vet material, either. A gust of wind could blow her over."

Bill popped his head over the stable door as Jake slid off the gray mare's bridle, replacing it with a head collar and tying her to the wall ring.

"According to Todd," Bill said, "she's very highly qualified and totally dedicated. If I'm honest, I suppose I felt a bit sorry for the lass. She seems lonely and I wanted to give her a break."

Jake picked up a body brush and began running it rhythmically across Carlotta's gleaming coat.

"Well, just keep her away from me."

"If she has any sense, she'll stay away from you all by herself," Bill retorted. "Oh, and by the way…"

Jake looked back, raising his eyebrows.

"I might have told her that you have some pups for sale."

"Well you'd better untell her, then, hadn't you," Jake snarled.

CHAPTER FIVE

DAWN WAS BREAKING as Cass pulled off the lane into the Low Fell parking lot. Rubbing her bleary eyes, she clambered out of her car, taking gulps of the sharp morning air to try and clear her head. In retrospect, the celebratory drink she and Clare had shared last night might have been a bit rash, since it had been almost midnight when she'd finally gotten to bed. Then again, she hadn't known she was to going to be called out to an emergency at five-thirty.

A small blue car was parked erratically, abandoned outside the clinic's front door. Cass peered around the courtyard—all she'd been told in the brief message she'd received half an hour ago was that a dog was having difficulties and its owner would bring it straight to the surgery. She heard a muffled sound beyond the bank of colorful begonias that lined the bright green grass at the side of the stone building.

"Hello!" she called, trying to make herself heard above the dawn chorus of a thousand early birds. "Can I help you?"

The woman who appeared from beyond the begonias was elderly, red-faced and very distraught. Cass recognized her at once. "Mrs. Park!" she exclaimed. "Is it Poppy?"

"Oh, thank God," the distressed old lady responded. "Yes…he's in the car."

A heavy lump settled in Cass's chest as she dug through her pocket for the surgery keys.

"Don't worry. We'll get him inside right away. What seems to be the problem?"

"He's choking on a chicken bone or something. He raided the garbage bin, you see."

Dropping her keys back into her pocket, Cass hurried toward the small car, flinging open the back door to see Poppy's smiling face eagerly awaiting her. When the little dog jumped out onto the tarmac and proceeded to run around in crazy circles,

Cass took a deep breath, trying to control her irritation.

"Mrs….er, Mary," she began. "I don't think…"

"Oh, you've saved him! However did you manage to do it so quickly?"

The sheer delight and admiration on the old lady's face dissolved Cass's anger instantaneously.

"But I didn't do anything,"

"So modest, as well," she added. "I must admit that, at first, I thought you looked far too young to be a vet. From now on, though, we will be singing your praises, won't we Poppy? That's twice you've saved my little precious in two days."

CASS RELATED THE incident to Donald later that morning. He let out a hoot of laughter, and suddenly she was laughing, too, feeling like a real part of the place.

"There you are, then," he announced. "You have your first adoring patient."

"Do you mean Mrs. Park or Poppy?" Cass giggled.

Just then, Todd strode into the room.

"If you're talking about my aunt, then

she's already been on the phone," he remarked, reaching for his white coat.

"Your aunt?" Cass echoed.

"Ah, so you'll know that Cass here is a miracle worker, then?" Donald said.

"But I didn't do anything," Cass insisted.

"Just enjoy the adulation," Todd suggested with a broad smile. "Knowing my Aunt Mary, she could well change her mind tomorrow. Now, on a more serious note, there's a call from Ben Naylor up at Hill Gate. Bad calving. Better get over there right away. Sally will give you directions."

"I'm on my way," Cass said, picking up her case.

Donald took hold of her arm as she passed by on her way to the door.

"About that dinner… Can you do tomorrow night?"

Cass nodded, smiling broadly.

"Thanks, that would be great."

THE BAD CALVING took longer than Cass had anticipated. Halfway through she almost called in for help, but thankfully the calf suddenly decided to greet the world. It slid from its mother, and Cass immediately began cleaning the mucus from the newborn's tiny nose, willing it to breathe as she rubbed its chest with a clump of straw. Elation flowed through her veins as the calf let out a low cry. There was something so special about bringing a new life into the world.

"Well done, lass," Ben Naylor remarked with begrudging surprise. "Frankly, when I saw you walk in, I considered telling you to get out. Slip of a thing like you! Todd told me there was no one else, though."

"You rang Todd?"

"Didn't think you were up to the job, to be honest."

She sat back on her heels, struggling to contain a surge of irritation. The middle-aged farmer stared back at her, his face open, and Cass couldn't help smiling.

"*Now* do you think I'm up to the job?"

He looked at the newborn calf, already struggling onto its tiny feet.

"Now," he said. "I'm going to get the missus to make us a nice cup of tea. Might be a slab of cake, as well, if you're lucky."

As Cass followed Ben Naylor across the yard to the gray stone farmhouse, she felt a warm sense of satisfaction. Today she'd proven herself to at least one member of the farming community. It was a start. And tonight she was taking her belongings over to Sky Cottage, her very own place. It felt like a turning point—a fresh start and a whole new life. She breathed in the country scents that filled the air around her—grass and flowers and always that underlying, heavy odor of cow muck. The smell that greeted her senses as she stepped through the kitchen door, however, made her mouth water.

"Come in, lass," urged Ben, ushering her ahead of him into the kitchen. "And meet my wife, Cathy."

Ben's wife was definitely not what Cass had expected. Small and dark and smartly dressed, Cathy moved quickly across the immaculate kitchen, shaking Cass's hand with a surprisingly firm grip.

"It's a nice change to have a female vet around here," she announced, smiling.

"When I was at vet school," Cass responded, "there were more than twice as many female students as males, so I guess you'll be seeing a lot more women vets in the future."

"Sign of the times," Ben grumbled. "Women are taking over the world."

"And about time, too," Cathy said brightly. "Especially around here. We're fifty years behind in these Lakeland hills. It's about time we joined the rest of the country. And Cass here did a good job, didn't she?"

"Well, that's true," Ben agreed. "It was a rough calving, too."

"So," Cathy asked, placing a pot of tea on the pine-topped table and motioning for Cass to sit down. "What made you decide to be a vet in the first place?"

Cass settled into a chair. "That's easy. I can pinpoint the exact day…well, almost. My parents had—have—a store in a busy village, and as a kid I spent a lot of time on my own, so they bought me a dog."

Cass hesitated, wondering why she was telling Cathy Naylor all this. Noting the interest in the woman's warm brown eyes, she went on.

"He was killed on the road when I was twelve years old, and when I realized I could have saved him if I'd known what to do, I decided to become a vet."

"What…just like that?"

Cass shrugged. "Pretty much, I guess."

Cathy set a plate heaped with homemade cakes onto the table and began pouring tea into three china mugs. "It seems to me that you must be a very determined and single-minded young woman."

Ben Naylor grinned, reaching for a muffin. "Bit like you, love," he said.

"Did you get another dog?" Cathy asked, ignoring him.

Cass shook her head.

"Well, now that you're settled into your new job, perhaps it's time you did. You're in the perfect situation, after all, and it'll keep you company. You can take it out with you on your visits, and—" a smile lit up her pleasant features "—at least you won't have any vet bills."

"There is that, I suppose." Cass laughed.

"Jake Munro has some puppies for sale," Ben said. "I saw them a couple of days ago when I called in at Sky View. Bonnie little black-and-tans, they are. Well-bred, too, if you ever fancy taking up shepherding."

"Thanks, but I wasn't really thinking of getting a sheepdog," Cass replied.

"You'd be surprised," insisted Ben. "Welsh Collies make good pets, as you know. They're trainable and loyal. You could do a lot worse. Jake's not the easiest man to deal with, of course, but it might be worth going to have a look at them."

Cass nodded thoughtfully. "I've already come across Mr. Munro, so I know exactly what you mean. I'm about to rent a cottage from his dad, actually."

Ben stood up, retrieving his cap. "Speak to Bill. He'll sort you out. Now I'd better go and get some work done. Oh…" He shifted from foot to foot. "Thanks for today."

"Glad to help." Cass smiled. "Perhaps you can spread the news around the farming community that I'm not totally useless."

"He'll certainly be doing that," Cathy declared.

Cass thought about going to see Jake Munro's puppies as she drove along the narrow lane. She dismissed the idea, concentrating hard on the road ahead. She'd hardly been in the area for two minutes—

better get herself settled first. And if she was going to get a dog, then perhaps it shouldn't come from the one person around here she hadn't hit it off with.

Way down below, she could see a line of slow-moving vehicles around the edge of the lake. The water shimmered, smooth as glass, then disappeared behind a wall of trees as she dropped down the hill. Everywhere she went here seemed to be either up or down. A vague longing for the open spaces of home brought a rush of nostalgia. It was months since she'd been back to the bustling village of St. Thomas to see her parents. She made a mental note to phone her mum.

Maybe this place would eventually come to feel like home. A warm glow settled over her as she remembered Ben Myers's appreciative handshake. At least now the farming community might begin to gain confidence in her ability to do her job.

AT SKY VIEW STABLES, Jake was heading for the house, his whole body aching with fatigue born of far more than just physical effort. As the kitchen door swung shut behind him, Bess, his loyal black-and-tan Welsh Collie, looked up at him adoringly. She was nursing her squirming brood of pups in a dog bed by the stove. The smallest puppy wriggled to the side of the bed, and she nudged it carefully back in beside her before looking back at Jake with shining eyes.

"You're a good mother, Bess," he told her, bending to scratch her ears. She squirmed in delight and he gave a wry smile. Straightening, he crossed the kitchen to flick on the kettle switch. The radio came on at the same time. Before he could turn it down, a deep male voice announced the next track.

And here's the number one song, 'Love me True,' from Tamara's long-awaited album of the same name."

Jake stood there, frozen, as Tara's throaty tones flooded into the room. It was as if the radio announcer had read his thoughts. A memory of her beautiful face filled his mind, bringing back memories…. Trouble was, all he'd seen back then was her beauty. He turned off the radio, welcoming silence, and for the millionth time, he wondered if things would have been different if Tara hadn't entered that singing competition.

His mother always tried to see the best in people, even finding a way to excuse Tara for walking out on him and the children. "She was going to leave eventually," Gwen had told him in the dark days after Tara had left them. "She's always been like a caged bird, and all you've really done is set her free. At least we still have Lucy and Robbie. That's the main thing.'

Another sharp pain tore into him as he remembered his ex-wife at the funeral, tall and elegant and oh-so-beautiful, holding Robbie's hand. He hadn't realized then that she was going to take the little boy away with her right after the funeral. During the reception at the house, she had packed a few of Robbie's toys and clothes while everyone else was downstairs, then she'd walked right out the front door with their son. She'd called Jake half an hour later, before he'd realized they were gone. She told him he wasn't fit to look after Robbie, compounding his guilt. Crushed by the weight of his loss, he hadn't been in a position to argue with her.

The house had felt so empty then. Anger had eaten at Jake's soul. He had been awarded custody of the twins after the divorce, but now Tara was threatening to get that decision overthrown. With the clever lawyers she had access to, anything was possible.

Eventually he closed the shutters, forcing his mind away from all the memories, shutting them out. He had totally messed up with his marriage, his kids and his whole life. Perhaps he deserved to suffer. Now he had no one, and that was how he wanted it. Loving someone laid you open to pain, as far as he could see. He was safer on his own, and perhaps Robbie was safer with his mother.

Something nudged Jake's hand—a cold, wet nose. He curled his fingers into Bess's coat. Sometimes love just crept up on you unexpectedly. That was what really scared him.

Through the window, Jake could see his father walking slowly across the yard. When had he begun to look so old? They lived in the same house, and yet they hardly even spoke. What was that all about? On a sudden impulse, Jake opened the window and leaned out.

"Coffee, Dad?"

The old man looked over at him in surprise, a smile lighting up his well-worn features.

"Yes...thanks, son. I'll be there in a minute."

BILL AND JAKE had become used to moving around the house in silence, getting on with their everyday lives without really communicating. Now they sat uneasily at the kitchen table, sipping strong coffee and watching Bess's pups wriggling out of their dog bed, missing the comfort of their mother's warmth and milk. Ignoring them, Bess sat at her master's feet.

The biggest pup, a bold black dog with a white line down his face, bounced across the floor toward his mother, and she sank onto her side, allowing him to nurse.

"Time you were finding homes for them," Bill remarked.

Jake nodded. "I've been asking around."

"As I already said, Cass is looking for a dog."

Jake looked up sharply, meeting his father's eyes. "Not that vet again?"

Bill sighed, draining his mug and slamming it down on the tabletop. "I don't know what you've got against her. It wasn't her fault about Rosie, and she'll be no bother as a tenant."

"It's not about Rosie."

"Well, what's it about, then?"

"She doesn't even look like a vet."

Bill smirked. "And what exactly is a vet supposed to look like?"

Jake shrugged, recognizing how lame his excuse sounded. "Well, definitely not like someone who could be blown over by a breath of wind."

"And definitely not beautiful, eh?" Bill said.

"She's hardly beautiful," Jake muttered. But he remembered the way he had felt when they first came face to face in the yard.... Was that why he had this compulsion to avoid her at all costs?

Bill stood up, shaking his head. "Okay, forget it. It was just a thought. You need to find homes for the pups, and she's looking for a dog. The way you feel about her has nothing to do with it."

"Oh, do what you want," Jake snapped. "Ask her if she wants a puppy, then, but keep her away from me."

"It seems to me that maybe she's made *too* much of an impression on you, son," Bill said. "All pretty girls aren't like Tara, you know."

"You mean *Tamara?* I just heard her new song on the radio."

"And you switched it right off, I suppose?"

Suddenly, Jake grinned. "Sure did. Don't get me wrong, Dad, I'm over her. It's just…"

"That you blame her for everything that's gone wrong in your life, and you miss Robbie desperately," Bill suggested. "Get onto that lawyer of yours again, or hire a different one."

An icy glint replaced the smile in Jake's blue eyes. "It's myself I blame. Anyway, Robbie is probably better off without me."

"Look, son…" Bill reached out his hand then drew it back again. "You've got to stop blaming yourself, and Robbie is definitely not better off without you."

For a moment, Jake held his father's gaze.

"Thanks, Dad," he responded, his voice tight with emotion. "Anyway, as I already said, if you want this...vet...to have a pup, then it's fine by me."

"Her name is Cass, and you could go and see her yourself."

With a snort of derision, Jake finished his coffee and stood up, stretching his arms above his head

"As if that's going to happen," he said, walking to the door.

CHAPTER SIX

CASS WAITED OUTSIDE the front door of the cottage, her heart playing racing games. This really was commitment, finally having her own place. Then again, she supposed, she was only renting. Real commitment was buying your own house—and having a husband and kids and the whole package. She stepped back, panic rising like a tide. What was happening to her? Perhaps she'd better just get back to the B and B and forget all about putting down roots.

She heard a vehicle approaching down the narrow grassy lane, and by the time Bill Munro's Land Rover appeared she had regained her composure. She was renting, that was all. Everyone had to have somewhere to live, and there was hardly anything too binding about a six-month lease.

The vehicle ground to a halt, and she

saw Bill's smiling face through the driver's door window. "Evening," he called, waving a key at her.

"Hi." She smiled back as he jumped out and headed for the front door.

He turned the old-fashioned key in the lock and the door swung open. "There you are then," he announced, ushering her inside. "Your new home. I'll leave you to get settled, but if there's anything you need, just call me."

Cass stepped into the cottage, breathing in the aroma of polish and the heady scent of the roses that grew around the front door.

"Thank you," she called as Bill walked back toward his vehicle.

He raised one hand. "No problem. We'll sort out the lease tomorrow. Oh, and…" He hung back. "If you still want a dog, you'll have to call in at the farm when you have time. Jake has some great little pups for sale. They're so cute you won't be able to resist them."

Cass wondered if now was the moment to tell him that she had decided not to get a dog just yet—and that she definitely didn't do cute. Did she look like the kind of girl who wanted cute?

Bill's Land Rover rattled into life, smoke from its exhaust floating up into the sweet summer air. The car disappeared around the corner, leaving behind a heavy silence and Cass stood in the doorway of her new home, breathing in her new life. After all the years of training and studying, was she actually here, in her own place, with a well-paid job and a career she loved?

Smiling broadly, Cass pinched herself hard on the arm. Yep, she really was here, and she was going to make herself so indispensable to the Low Fell Animal Clinic that they'd never want to let her go. Picking up her suitcase, she stepped into the hallway. Now, where to start?

AFTER ALL THE excitement of moving into the cottage and the satisfaction of the calving at the Naylors' place, Cass found the morning clinic the following day quite mundane. There was nothing she couldn't handle—apart from an overweight, middle-aged man who wanted to complain about his bill. She steered him in Todd's direction.

"Thanks for that," Todd said, popping his head around the door after the man had left. "He does that every month's end. Brings in Rover with an imaginary problem and then starts to complain about the cost."

"It's called Spot." Cass laughed. "And it really did have a tick on its head."

"I hear that you've rented Bill Munro's cottage," Todd said, changing the subject. "Settling in okay?"

"Last night was my first night there, so I've hardly settled in, but I love it already."

"And you don't mind the isolation?"

She hesitated, considering her reply.

"No, not at all.... I like being on my own."

"But you do have family?"

"Oh, yes. There's just me and my parents, no siblings, so I got used to my own company when I was a kid."

He nodded. "You'll certainly be on your own at the cottage. I hope you enjoy it there."

"I will," Cass insisted. "It's so beautiful around here."

"It gets pretty bleak in the winter, though. You may want to think about getting a four-by-four."

A warm glow spread through Cass's body. If Todd was talking about her future at the practice, then he must think she was doing a good job.

"Thanks," she said. "I might just do that."

Cass was still smiling inside half an hour later as she hung up her white coat and reached for her jacket. Tonight she was going to Donald's for dinner. His wife, Jenny, had sounded lovely on the phone and made her feel so welcome. It felt good to be making friends here, as if she really did belong.

As if on cue, as she walked toward her car jangling her keys, Donald appeared, walking hurriedly across the parking lot.

"You're still coming tonight, aren't you?" he asked. "I already have loads of visits to make, and Todd asked me to call in at Pat O'Neill's to check on one of his patients— a gray mare with an abscess on her jaw. I hope I'm not too late getting home. If I am, you'll have to make my excuses to Jenny. You do know where we are, I suppose?"

Cass nodded. "Yes, thanks. Jenny gave me directions. I'll see you later, then."

"Looking forward to it," Donald said. "If I ever get finished, that is. And don't forget…"

"I know," Cass said, unlocking her car. "Make your excuses to Jenny if you're late. Although I'm sure she must be used to a vet's unpredictable hours by now."

JAKE RUSHED OUT of the house as soon as he heard Donald's four-by-four grind to a halt in the yard.

He knew the vet had likely been on his way home when he'd called, but one of the youngsters had ripped a chunk out of its bottom lip, and Jake didn't think it could wait.

"It's the bay colt," he announced, already striding toward the barn.

"What has he done this time?" Donald groaned. "That colt is the most accident-prone animal I've ever met."

The torn lip was messy but not serious,

he told Jake, after a quick inspection of the wound. He reached for his bag, glancing up at Jake in relief.

"I'll clean it up, but here's not much more I can do. When his lip's had the chance to dry, I can easily remove that dangly bit of flesh."

Jake nodded. "That's what I thought, but he needed a shot of antibiotic anyway."

With a final pat to the elegant youngster's satiny neck, Jake followed the vet out into the yard.

"Thanks for coming so quickly," he said. "I hope I haven't made you late."

Donald smiled. "Tell you what," he said. "Why don't you come over for a meal tonight? It will do you good to get out, and we can look over that stallion's paperwork. You remember, I mentioned him the other day—Bob Nelson's new acquisition, Grand Design. He's a lovely Thoroughbred with superb conformation."

Jake felt a prickle of interest as he contemplated the invitation.

"Have you seen him?"

Donald nodded. "Yes, and he's one of

the nicest horses I've seen in years. I have some pictures and all his information."

"Okay, thanks then," Jake said. "When do you want me?"

Donald glanced uneasily at his watch.

"As soon as you can. I should have been home half an hour ago."

Twenty minutes later, Jake was staring at his reflection in the bathroom mirror. He pressed a tissue against a dark blot of red that marked his chin, wincing. Why had he agreed to go to Donald's anyway? He had better things to do with his time. Remembering the vet's mention of the new stud, however, he brightened. It would be good to talk horses all night, and Jake was on the lookout for a top stallion to put Carlotta to next spring. Her foal would be the best thing to happen around here in a long while. Jake washed his face and rubbed it dry, then reached for his shirt. Suddenly, he was looking forward to an evening spent talking horses. Bill was in the kitchen when Jake went back downstairs, watching the small TV on the wall and playing with one of Bess's pups.

"It's nice to see you going out for once,

son," he remarked. "Oh, and by the way, if it's all right with you, I've given this puppy a name. I know I shouldn't have, since you aren't keeping any, but when I let them out in the yard earlier I found her upside down in a puddle."

Jake couldn't help smiling.. "One, I am going out on business, and two, how does being in a puddle of water suggest a good name for a dog?"

"Well, that's just it. That's her name—Puddle."

"You can't call a dog Puddle."

"I just did," Bill said with a broad grin. "Anyway, it's only until she gets a new home. I'm sure her future owners will want to choose their own name."

The pup, Jake realized, was a miniature replica of Bess. He watched as she chewed determinedly on his dad's shoelaces, and suddenly the vague idea that had been running around inside his head turned into a decision.

"Well, maybe your daft name will have to stick. I was thinking of keeping this one."

"Puddle it is then." Bill looked up at his

son in delight. "So you *do* still have a softer side."

"Pure common sense, that's all," Jake said. "Poor old Bess can't go on forever, and we have to have a dog to herd sheep."

At the sound of her name, Bess padded across to her master and pushed her cold nose into his hand.

"Anyway," he murmured, scratching her behind the ears. "She's Bess's favorite."

"And yours," Bill added softly, as the kitchen door banged shut behind him.

CASS WALKED NERVOUSLY down the path toward the Darwens' quaint country cottage, smoothing down her skirt and feeling self-conscious. She didn't normally wear dresses, but tonight felt a bit like a celebration. Celebrations, she had decided, required extra effort. The little black number she'd wriggled into, however, had definitely been a mistake. She should have worn something much more country and understated.

She did a quick U-turn. She still had enough time to nip home and change without anyone being the wiser. Her blue jeans should be dry by now, and she could wear that red and white checked shirt.

The warm tones of a woman's voice stopped her in her tracks and she turned around. Jenny Darwen tossed back a lock of blond hair and held out her hand.

"Hi, you must be Cass."

"Sorry," Cass said awkwardly. "I think I forgot to lock my car...and you must be Jenny."

The woman nodded, smiling, and Cass shook her hand briefly while pulling out her key. She felt even more self-conscious as she pressed the lock button.

"I must have done it, after all," she mumbled.

"Come inside and meet the brood," Jenny urged.

The Darwens' cottage was warm and homey—a perfect place for a family, Cass thought as Jenny ushered her into the living room.

"Ollie and Evie," she announced proudly, as two tiny versions of herself turned from the TV to stare at the new arrival. "Ollie is four and Evie's three as of last week. Say hello, kids."

"They're gorgeous," Cass said, dropping down to their level. "Hello, you two, what are you watching?"

Two solemn sets of wide eyes met hers and turned immediately back to the cartoon characters flickering across the screen.

Jenny laughed. "Don't mind them—they love this show. Don should be back any minute. He's late again—as usual."

"Goes with the territory, I'm afraid," Cass said, standing up and smoothing down her skirt again. Oh, how she wished she'd worn jeans. What had she been thinking? "Can I do anything to help?" she offered.

"No, thanks. I have everything covered. Just the kids to put to bed. I was keeping them awake to see their dad, but…" Jenny shrugged, picking up Evie and calling for Ollie. "Come on, bedtime."

"I could read them a story, if you like," Cass suggested. "I haven't had much experience with children, but I'm sure I could manage that."

"Well, if you don't mind…. They do love being read to."

Cass reached for Ollie's small hand,

and when he closed his chubby fingers around hers she felt an unexpected trickle of warmth and emotion. She took a deep breath. She had her career to focus on, and even if having a family figured into her future, she knew the demands of an equestrian specialty would leave her with little time to devote to children or a husband. Nothing like the attention Jenny gave Ollie and Evie. And anyway, she liked her independence. ...

"I'd be happy to," she said.

Ollie and little Evie snuggled into their beds, eyes bright with anticipation as Cass knelt on the floor between them and opened a large, colorful story book.

"Once upon a time..."

JAKE DROVE SLOWLY along the lane toward the Darwens' cottage, wondering for the umpteenth time why he had agreed to Donald's invitation. He reminded himself that he would love to get more information about Bob Nelson's new stallion, and Jenny always made him very welcome. Suddenly, he was looking forward to the visit.

It wasn't until he was out of his vehicle and approaching the front door that he noticed another other car parked outside. Surely it couldn't be...

"Jake," Donald called. "Come on in. You're just in time to help me explain my lateness."

"Just blame me," Jake said. "After all, it was my fault."

"So he *was* telling the truth." Jenny laughed, appearing from behind her husband. "Glad you could come, Jake, and don't worry—I've been a vet's wife for far too long to expect him to stay on schedule."

Donald gave her a hug, lifting her off the ground and swinging her around.

"This is what you need, Jake," he exclaimed. "A Jenny, like mine."

"I don't think they're too easily come by." Jake warmed to the moment, forgetting all about the car.

"That," said Donald, "is because she's unique."

"Okay, you don't need to do any more sucking up," Jenny retorted, cheeks glowing. "Let's go inside."

While Donald went to get changed and Jenny disappeared into the kitchen, Jake sipped the beer she'd brought him, flipping idly through the latest issue of *Horse and Hound*. The aromas wafting in from the kitchen made him realize just how hungry he was. Closing the magazine, he wandered in to see if he could be of any help.

As he crossed the hall, he sensed a movement on the stairs. He looked up expecting to see Donald and found himself transfixed by smooth, slim brown legs. His gaze lingered involuntarily before sliding awkwardly away.

"THEY'RE ASLEEP, JENNY," Cass began, her voice dying out as she saw Jake's tall figure below her. For an endless moment, it felt like their first encounter all over again. She shuddered as their eyes met and her hands slid involuntarily toward her hemline. "Oh," she managed. "It's you."

Jake cleared his throat, anger rising inside him—anger at Donald for setting him up, anger at Cass for being there and anger at himself for reacting.

"Donald didn't say you would be here."

Cass bristled at the animosity in his voice, all self-consciousness vanishing.

"Hello to you, too. He didn't say you'd be here, either." She ran lightly down the stairs and stood in front of him, drawing herself up as tall as she could, barely reaching his shoulders. "So, I'm guessing you wouldn't have come if you'd known."

He caught her gaze and immediately looked away again, focusing on the top of her head.

"I don't care if you're here or not," he told her. "Donald and I have some business…"

"And what business might that be?" Donald's pleasant voice held a hint of amusement, but when they both looked up to where he stood on the staircase, his expression appeared totally serious.

A flush colored Jake's tanned skin. "The stallion. We were going to go through his details, remember?"

Donald's face lit up with customary good humor as he joined them in the hallway. "Don't worry, I haven't forgotten. Let's eat first though, eh?"

CASS WISHED JENNY hadn't seated her right across from Jake. She felt as if he was watching her every mouthful, waiting for her to spill soup on the tablecloth or drip cheese down her chin. She ate slowly, looking anywhere except into those cold blue eyes.

"How has work been, Cass?" Donald asked, clearly trying to break the tension. "Winning those farmers over yet?"

She smiled, remembering the successful calving. "Well, one at least," she replied, deliberately catching Jake's eye. "Ben Naylor has decided I'm okay."

"Did he take you into the kitchen, introduce you to the lovely Cathy and supply you with tea and scones?"

Cass giggled. "Something like that."

"Then believe you me," Donald said, standing up to replenish the wine glasses. "You've won him over. In fact, let's have a toast." Raising his glass he looked pointedly at Jake. "To Cass's success!"

Seemingly unaware of the tension, Jenny laughed, joining in. "To Cass."

Jake lifted his glass in a half-hearted motion before placing it back on the table, glancing up suddenly to meet Cass's warm brown eyes. He expected to find triumph in her face, but all he saw was softness.

"My dad mentioned that you'd like a dog," he heard himself say. "I do have some pups, but there's only one left. A black dog with a white line down its face…"

"Thanks." Cass smiled. "I'll think about it. I'm not sure if I'm ready to be a dog owner yet, though. I suppose I should really get myself settled first."

Jake shrugged, regretting his offer. "Suit yourself. It won't be there for long, though."

CHAPTER SEVEN

CASS WONDERED HOW she had allowed herself to be persuaded to go and see Jake Munro's puppy tomorrow. She'd tried to explain again, to Donald and Jenny, that she wasn't ready for the commitment of a dog. Neither of them had taken any notice of her, of course.

"You need a companion, living all on your own now," Jenny insisted.

"And you're in the perfect position, after all," Donald added. "You can bring it to work every day—Todd won't mind, he's a real dog lover."

"Like his aunt." Cass smiled.

"Don't tell me you've met the estimable Poppy already," Donald said, chuckling.

"He's my new best friend," Cass replied.

Cass felt laughter bubbling inside her. She couldn't remember when she'd had such a good time or felt so relaxed with relative strangers—discounting Jake, of course. After his unexpected offer, he had withdrawn from their company and immersed himself in the stud information Donald had finally provided. Believing he must have regretted his impulsive gesture, Cass decided to broach the subject again.

Donald had disappeared upstairs and Jenny was in the kitchen when Cass found her moment. She stepped determinedly into Donald's small office, speaking to the back of Jake's head. His brown hair curled over his collar, she noted, and his checked shirt could have done with some ironing.

"Look," she began. "I'm well aware that you and I haven't really hit it off, so I understand if you'd rather I didn't come and see the pups. As I said, I'm not really ready to get one yet."

Jake swung around to face her, a deep frown lining his forehead. "Whatever," he said, shrugging. "It doesn't matter to me. There's only one left without a home, anyway. And it'll be my dad who sees you."

"Oh, right."

Feeling totally dismissed, Cass turned away abruptly, but Jake's deep voice followed her. "Sorry..." She looked back at him. Had he really said that? The slope of his shoulders betrayed an unexpected vulnerability, throwing her off guard and evaporating her irritation.

"It's just..." He stood, holding her eyes. "I don't really do company."

"That's okay," she smiled. "Neither do I, usually."

CASS WAS STILL thinking about Jake Munro as she turned her key in the lock at Sky Cottage and flicked on the light. Obviously, he'd been trying to overcome tragedy in his life—but so had Bill. Unlike his son, Bill was really friendly. Jake seemed to have a darkness to him, as if all emotion had been drained from his soul. Cass couldn't help wondering if he had always been that way.

Despite the late hour, Cass didn't feel like sleeping. She sat for a while, reflecting on her evening, and dozed off in her chair, waking with a start to her phone vibrating against her hip. She shook herself awake groggily.

"Hi, Cass here," she answered.

Todd's strong tones burst into her ear.

"Emergency. Sorry, I know you aren't on call, but I could really do with a hand at the clinic. Unless you're busy?"

Her bag hit the floor with a thump as she headed for the stairs.

"I'm on my way."

It hadn't occurred to Cass to ask what the emergency was. An animal needed help— that was enough. She drove along the grassy lane, peering over the steering wheel to follow the channel of bright light from her high beams. Beyond it, the night was as black as ink.

The figure appeared unexpectedly, stopping the breath in her throat. Who would be walking around at this time of night? She swerved to avoid what she hoped was a real person and not some kind of wandering spirit. She spun her wheel, and as the figure moved back into the hedge, her lights picked out his face. *Jake Munro*. Was the man insane? She drove on, refusing to allow him to spook her. It wasn't a ghost after all, just her stupid, deranged neighbor—and was that a dog he had at his heels?

JAKE LEFT DONALD'S cottage soon after Cass, his thoughts full of the stallion he and Donald had eventually got around to discussing. Grand Design—the name definitely had a ring to it. Carlotta's foal would be a new hope for the future, a step forward when everything felt like it was behind him. But as he drove home, his demons came back to haunt him, suffocating his ambition. What was he thinking? He had lost his right to a future over twelve months ago.

Discarding his vehicle on the drive outside Sky View, Jake went to check on the horses. Carlotta's pale head was over her half door, revealed by the moonlight. She snuffled against his hand, looking for a tidbit. "Would you like to have a foal, girl?" he murmured, the familiar aroma of horse bringing a kind of comfort. For a fleeting moment, his heart lifted as hopes and dreams rushed back in. No! He turned away, striding across the yard, hands thrust deep in his pockets. There was no longer a place in his life for dreams.

WOKEN BY A FRANTIC scratching sound, Bill Munro rubbed his eyes and clambered wearily from his bed. "What's up, lass?" he called, easing his aching bones as he made his way carefully down the stairs.

Below him, in the hallway, he could see Bess by the door. Nose lowered to the crack at the bottom, she sniffed and scratched in a frenzy, stopping for a moment to gaze up at the old man appealingly.

"Left your pups for once then, eh lass? I guess it really is time for them to find new homes. Now, what are you after? Is it rats?"

Bill opened the door and peered outside, breathing in the clear night air and narrowing his eyes to adjust to the darkness. Something moved by Carlotta's stable, and Jake's tall shape emerged from the shadows, an isolated figure in the moonlight. Bess pushed urgently against Bill's legs. He stood back to let her through, watching as she raced off across the yard toward her master. "Go keep him company, lass," he murmured. "Someone sure needs to."

He could see Jake's hand drop down in a brief caress as the dog slipped up behind him, but when his eyes remained firmly fixed on the horizon, a knot of sadness tightened in Bill's chest. "Life goes on, lad," he said softly, feeling his son's pain. "And you'll have to learn to go with it…or tear yourself apart."

JAKE WALKED ON AUTOPILOT, his mind taken up by memories, each jostling for first place. Poor old Rosie, his last link with Lucy, her huge, kind eyes glazed over in death; his mother's smiling face on the morning he set off for the show in Holland. She had waved frantically, he remembered, as the truck rolled away. Had he even kissed her goodbye?

And then there was Tara. She had always been a free spirit—that was what Jake had most liked about her when they first met, her single-minded ferocity for life. Now he saw it only as selfishness. Then again, who was he to call anyone selfish?

Stopping suddenly, he reached down to cradle Bess's head between his palms, allowing himself to think about Robbie for a moment. To lose both his daughter and his mother had been unbearable, but to then lose his five-year-old son had taken away every reason for living. He had tried to stay strong for Robbie in the days after the tragedy, bottling up all the agony and guilt when the little boy was around. And he had even been relieved when Tara had arrived to lend her support. But why hadn't he realized that Tara planned to steal Robbie away as soon as Gwen and Lucy were laid to rest?

When he found out that Tara was taking Robbie back to America with her, it felt as if a black hole had opened up and swallowed his whole world. Maybe Tara was right to say he wasn't fit to look after their son. He should have been more vigilant… should have been a better dad.

Clenching his jaw, Jake stood up. That was all in the past, buried with the rest of his heartache.

"Come on, girl," he called, his voice echoing in the emptiness of the night as he headed toward the gate that led onto the steep incline of the Lakeland fell.

Jake saw the lights heading toward him just as he reached the curve in the lane, near the path to Sky Cottage. Bess slid in behind his legs as he stepped back into the hedge, and he linked a finger beneath her collar as a car came into view. A white face peered over the steering wheel. Wide eyes stared at him in alarm. The vet! Of course it was the vet again. Could he never get away from her?

CASS'S FINGERS FROZE on the wheel as she regained control of her car. Did Jake Munro make a habit of wandering around in the dead of night? At Donald's, earlier that evening, he had seemed almost normal—a bit morose and kind of surly, but eloquent enough, at least when he was talking to Donald. She had overheard them in the study after dinner, getting all excited about bloodlines.

CASS SWERVED INTO the parking lot focusing on the job at hand. Todd hadn't said what the emergency was, but based on the abandoned livestock trailer and four-by-four in the lot, it was pretty apparent that something a little larger than a dog or cat needed treatment.

Lights blazed from the windows, illuminating her path as she raced toward the large animal unit at the back of the building. She found an elderly farmer hanging onto the lead rope of a wild Fell pony while Todd examined its belly.

"Oh, good, you're here," her boss remarked without looking over at her. "We're going to need to sedate her. She has some nasty lacerations right across her stomach from trying to jump a barbed wire fence. This is Raymond Johnston, by the way."

"She did jump it," Raymond cut in, nodding at Cass. "I brought four of them in from the fell this afternoon, for the sale at Kirby Stephen on Saturday. The other three were fine, but Belle here decided to hightail it back to the rest of the herd just as it was getting dark. Trouble is, the fence she jumped led into the lane. Two miles, she went, before we managed to herd her into the farmyard at Borrans. It was only then that I realized what a mess she'd made of herself. I went home to get the trailer and it took another couple of hours to get her loaded. It seemed sensible just to bring her straight here."

"Wise move," Todd said.

Sedating the filly was a lot harder than Cass had expected.

"They're so wild, these ponies," Todd

explained, struggling for a vein as they tried to keep her still. "You can give them enough drugs to take down an elephant, and they'll fight it off. That's the worry—you can overdo it."

With a gasp of relief, Todd stood back. "There. We'll leave her to settle for a while, give the anesthetic a chance to kick in."

The filly cowered against the wall, straining against her head collar, sides heaving and eyes wild with panic.

"Hey girl," Cass murmured, crooning softly under her breath. "You're going to be fine."

"Has she been handled at all, Ray?" asked Todd.

The filly's elderly owner shrugged. "Not really. They usually come around easily enough, once we get them down from the fell. This one seems to be the exception, though."

"You might say that," Todd agreed checking on the youngster. "Well," he exclaimed. "Would you look at that?"

Cass stood right next to the black fell pony, crooning in the same melodic tone as she ran her hand gently across its sweat-marked coat. The wildness in the terrified creature's eyes faded, and her whole body quivered softly. Feeling Todd's eyes on her, Cass glanced up, meeting his gaze with a gentle smile.

"She's calmed down a bit now."

Todd jumped into action.

"That's great. You just keep right on with whatever it is you're doing and I'll get started."

IT WAS ALMOST an hour before Todd announced the cleaning and suturing done to his satisfaction. The filly stood head down and forelegs splayed. Ray Johnston's weathered face cracked into a thousand tiny lines.

"Good job, that," he declared.

Todd surveyed his handiwork, standing back, pleased with the result. "Plenty of antibiotics, and hopefully she'll be as good as new in no time," he said, looking curiously across at Cass. "And why didn't you tell me you had such a way with horses?"

Cass shrugged. "To be honest, I've never really had all that much to do with them. At least not until I started my training. I just love them, I guess, and they seem to sense that."

"Sign of a true horsewoman," Todd said. "I'll have to put more equestrian work your way."

"Well…" Anticipation prickled as Cass digested his words. "I wouldn't like to step on Donald's toes, but working *with* him would be brilliant."

"I'll bear that in mind," Todd promised. "Now Ray, you may as well get off. You can come and collect the pony in the morning."

After Cass and Todd had finished cleaning up, she went back to check on the filly, determined not to leave until she was settled. Todd appeared behind her with a steaming mug of tea, and she took it gratefully. "It's been quite a night, eh?" he remarked. "Thanks for the assistance."

"I've enjoyed helping," she said. "The poor little thing was so scared."

He nodded "A lot of the farmers around here breed Fell ponies. They're so hardy that the farmers usually leave them to their own devices until they're three years old and they can take them to auction."

"I've never been to a horse auction."

"Well, when you go to Jake Munro's to-morrow, why don't you ask him if you can tag along this Saturday? He's sure to be going."

Cass frowned. "How did you know about me going to Sky View?"

"Nothing gets by me."

"I'm beginning to realize that, but I can't see *Mr.* Munro inviting me anywhere, can you? I'm not exactly his favorite person."

"Jake's all right, really," Todd said. "He just can't get past the tragedy. Blames him-self, I suppose."

"For his little girl's accident? But why? It wasn't his fault."

"No, but when something like that hap-pens, I guess you always blame yourself. You know—'what if?' Jake was often away around then, you see, competing."

"And did he do well?"

"He was one of the best. Gave it all up after the accident, though. He did carry on competing after his wife left him, travel-ling all over Europe while his kids stayed with his parents."

"So that's why he moved back home?"

"Yes. His wife won some competition and went off to be a singer. She's done really well, too. You must have heard of her—Tamara?"

"Tamara!" Cass cried. "You mean *the* Tamara? I love her music."

"She has a lovely voice," Todd agreed. "They didn't live around here then, so none of us really knew her. Jake had a stable yard down South. After she won the competition, she just up and left, leaving their twins with Jake. He moved back here and threw himself into his career. Gwen and Bill didn't mind—they loved having him back, and they loved taking care of the children. The accident happened one winter morning. You know, late for school, patch of ice. Jake gave up on everything after that. And his ex taking their little boy to live with her in America made things even worse."

A lump settled in Cass's chest.

"Poor guy. No wonder he's so dark."

"Dark certainly describes him. He wouldn't thank you for your sympathy, though. You're off on Saturday, so why don't you ask him for a lift to the sale. It might be good for him, a bit of female company."

"Not mine, I'm afraid," Cass said, reaching for her coat. "Though I would love to go."

"Well then, go for it," Todd said. "He doesn't bite."

She laughed uneasily, remembering Jake's shadowy figure in the lane. "Are you sure about that?"

CHAPTER EIGHT

IT WAS A lovely night for a walk, Cass thought as she set off for Sky View. The evening sun hung in the sky, a glorious golden orb tinged with rose. The scent of freshly cut grass lingered in the light breeze, far sweeter than the most expensive perfume in the world. She breathed deeply, absorbing the scenery around her and realizing how much she had come to love this place already. It felt as if this was finally where she was supposed to be.

Glancing at her watch, she quickened her steps. Bill had asked her to be there at seven, and it was almost five past already. Her stomach churned as she opened the gate into the stable yard, closing it carefully behind her before heading for the house. Could she really cope with a puppy, if she did decide to get one? Taking it to work every day and caring for it 24/7? Being responsible for another living thing was a big task, especially since she'd spent most of her life thinking about herself. Perhaps she was selfish—or self-absorbed, at least. Maybe she needed something to care for. Guilt stabbed deep. She really must find time to go see her parents soon.

The door opened just as she raised her hand to knock.

"Ah, you're here," Bill said with a broad smile.

"Sorry I'm a bit late," she began.

He held up his hand, cutting short her apologies. "Don't worry about it. I know how busy you veterinarians get."

"I wasn't busy," she admitted. "To be honest, I got wrapped up in the scenery on my walk over here."

"Well, it is pretty stunning," Bill agreed, ushering her inside.

As Cass stepped into the disarray of the large farmhouse kitchen, a black nose appeared in the doorway ahead, closely followed by four more. Suddenly, she was surrounded by five squirming balls of fluff whining for her attention.

"Bess must be with Jake," Bill said. "She's been going off and leaving them a lot lately, so I don't reckon she'll miss them too much when they go."

The biggest puppy, a black dog with a white line down its face, barked at Cass's feet, head lowered to its paws and tail wagging madly. Laughing, she picked it up.

"You," she said, "must be the ringleader. I presume he's the one who hasn't got a home yet."

"Sure is. He's been nothing but trouble since he first opened his eyes. Still, the only reason he hasn't been taken is because most farmers want females."

"Are they all going to farmers?"

"Mostly. They'll make good sheep dogs."

"So it wouldn't really be fair to have them as pets?" Cass asked.

"Oh no, that's not a problem. They'll make good pets, too—as long as they get plenty of exercise. Here…" Bill picked up a black and tan puppy, the smallest of the brood, and placed it into Cass's arms. "This is Puddle."

She looked up at her with sweet, dark eyes, and Cass felt her heart melt.

"She is so cute," she said with a sigh. "And who named her Puddle?"

Bill laughed. "I did."

Cass cuddled the pup against her chest.

"Unfortunately, I'm afraid that Puddle here isn't for sale. Jake has decided to keep her."

Cass felt an unexpected lurch of disappointment.

"I don't suppose he could be persuaded to let her go?" she asked hopefully.

Bill shook his head. "I doubt it…she looks like her mother, you see."

"She does, doesn't she? How'd she get her name, anyway?"

"She snuck into the yard and I found her in a puddle of water. She's a real wanderer, and…" Bill paused midsentence as the kitchen door opened, revealing Jake's tall figure. "Cass is here to see the pups," he announced.

Jake hesitated, his expression awkward. He seemed to fill the whole room. "I can see that," he said, glancing across at her. "I didn't realize you were already here."

PLACING PUDDLE CAREFULLY back with her siblings, Cass smiled in Jake's general direction.

"It's okay, I'm about to leave."

"Cass here has fallen in love with Puddle," Bill said.

A spontaneous smile flitted across Jake's face. "Daft name that," he remarked, catching Cass's eye. "Nothing to do with me, I might add."

"Well, it's certainly different," she agreed. "Your dad tells me you're keeping her."

"Yes. She's the image of her mum." He reached down to scratch Bess's head. "The black pup is still looking for a home."

Cass picked up her bag.

"He's lovely, and I really will think about it. Thanks for showing them to me."

Jake's response was totally unexpected.

"Dogs are good company you know—undemanding and affectionate."

Cass raised her eyebrows, holding back a smile. "And people aren't?"

Jake grimaced. "Well, now that you mention it…"

"You're so cynical," she couldn't help adding.

A flicker of humor lightened his features. "Ah, you noticed. I've had a lot of practice."

Remembering Todd's advice and realizing that now was the only chance she might get, Cass took a deep breath. "By the way, I...I have a favor to ask."

JAKE LOOKED AROUND the room as though expecting to see someone else. "Of me...?"

"Well, yes. It's not much, really. I was hoping to go to the horse sale on Saturday and I wondered if you could..."

Suddenly the thought of spending an hour alone with Jake, trying to make conversation, seemed too daunting.

"Give me directions," she finished. "You know, just to make sure I get to the right place."

"Perhaps you could give her a lift," Bill suggested.

Jake scowled. "I haven't decided what time I'm going, and I have something to do after..."

"It's fine," Cass insisted, feeling her cheeks burn. "I don't need a ride."

"Well, you don't need me, either. Dad can tell you how to get there."

He turned on his heel and disappeared into the yard.

"Sorry about Jake," Bill apologized. "I'll get some paper to write down those directions. Sure you don't want to change your mind about the pup?"

Cass shook her head.

"He's lovely, but he seems a bit big and boisterous. After meeting Puddle…I don't suppose Jake could be persuaded to change his mind about keeping her?"

"Not much chance of that, I'm afraid."

"I didn't think so. You aren't going to the sale, then?"

Bill frowned. "I hadn't really thought about it, to be honest. I do go occasionally. Jake, now, he never misses one."

"Does he always buy?"

"Sometimes, if he sees a youngster that strikes him as promising. He bought the skinniest, plainest filly last year, and she turned out to be a real head-turner. He's good at that, you know— seeing through them."

"It doesn't follow with people, then?" Cass heard the words tumble from her lips and could have kicked herself.

Bill just smiled. "No, I guess not. He

certainly couldn't see through Tara.... I'll go find that paper."

As he left the room, Cass found herself wishing she'd known Jake before his whole world came tumbling down around him. What kind of man was he then?

The thought was still circling inside her head as she walked slowly back toward her cottage. Waste of time wondering, she told herself. She would never know.

CHAPTER NINE

"ARE YOU GOING, THEN?" Todd asked, bursting into the consulting room from his office just as Cass's final patient, a three-legged German shepherd, left with his diminutive owner.

"Bye, Mrs. Carlisle, and don't worry, Butch is going to be fine," she called, before turning to her boss with a smile.

"I thought dogs were supposed to look like their owners. Anyway, what do you mean? Going where?"

"Kirby sale, tomorrow. You were going to ask Jake Munro for a lift, remember? Got cold feet, eh?"

Cass shrugged. "No, actually. To be honest, I couldn't handle the thought of spending all that time in his company—even if he'd said yes, which would have been highly unlikely. I might go myself, though."

"Good idea. If you really are serious about doing more equestrian work, then the more you experience the better. Horse owners want their vets to be knowledgeable."

"I am serious about it," Cass said firmly. "I'd like to take riding lessons, too."

"Now that is an excellent plan. I would suggest you ask Jake, but I guess that's a no, too."

"What do you think?" Cass said with a laugh.

Cass set off for the sale at six-thirty the next morning. Her sleep had been restless, filled with dreams of galloping horses, icy blue eyes and a huge dark shadow of anger that turned into a real and tangible thing, threatening to engulf her.

She felt bleary-eyed and slow as she headed for her car. The sharp morning air brought a fresh clarity, however, and as she started the engine she found herself looking forward to the new experience.

Finding Kirby Stephen was easy, thanks to Bill's scrawled directions, but once she'd arrived on the main street of the busy mar-

ket town, Cass couldn't find the entrance
to the sale. However, she soon realized all
she had to do was follow a horse trailer.
Where else would it be going?

She had believed herself to be reason-
ably early, but already the whole auction
was teeming with color and sound—horses
being trotted out across the parking lot as
dealers tried to make a purchase before the
sale began; terrified whinnies from youngsters herded straight down from the fell;
and the distinctive aroma of horse sweat
and dung.

She parked her car and hurried eagerly
toward the holding pens near the sale room,
carried along on the wave of excitement
that seemed to hang in the air. She noticed
Ray Johnston almost immediately, leaning against the rails of a pen packed with
nervous-looking black Fell ponies. Steam
rose above him in a cloud as he tried to
calm them.

"Ah," he called, spotting her. "It's you."

"Call me Cass." She smiled. "When will
they go through the ring?"

"Oh, it'll be ages yet. I'm just trying to
get these numbers on their backsides."

"I'll give you a hand…"

The offer was impulsive, but as she made it, Cass was suddenly aware that she really did want to be involved. She felt desperately sorry for the half-wild ponies, but her job was to help, not judge. If this was the way these local farmers worked, then she needed to understand what went on and try to make things better.

Ray's expression was wary.

"I'll not be paying you," he told her.

"Don't worry, I'm not on duty." She laughed. "Now, I'll try to keep them still while you put on those stickers."

The unexpected skill Cass had previously discovered, her instinctive ability to communicate with horses, was not nearly as apparent in the chaos of the sales. There was too much adrenaline around for her to get the full attention of the anxious ponies, but she did manage to keep them calm long enough for Ray to put the numbers on their rumps.

"There," he announced, standing back. "That's it. Thanks."

The ponies huddled in a corner of their pen, pressing against each other. Cass thought there was something very sad about the black-and-white markers. No names, just numbers.

"How's Belle doing?" she asked, relieved that she, at least, had escaped the sale ring.

"She's healing okay. I may as well put her in foal now that she's staying a bit longer. I was trying to cut back, but obviously I can't sell her anymore, and there's no point in feeding a horse for nothing."

Ray's comment gave Cass a renewed awareness of the Lakeland farmers' way of working. They took care of their animals, but tried not to get sentimentally attached, even though it was obvious that they sometimes did. Money was tight, and all stock had to earn its keep. There was no room for hangers on.

"I'm going to have a look around, then," Cass said.

Ray nodded. "Thanks again for the help. And they'll be okay, you know—the ponies. They usually end up selling to someone to break and sell on as riding ponies, or to drive, even. You'd be surprised how quickly they settle once they've been handled a bit more."

Cass smiled, grateful for his reassurance. "Glad to hear that," she said, meaning it.

JAKE NOTICED THE GLEAMING sweep of Cass's dark hair from across a row of pens, recognizing her immediately. So she'd been serious about coming to the sale, then. But why was she talking to Ray Johnston?

She turned in his direction, and he averted his gaze. When she stopped again, to peer over the rails at a leggy bay, his eyes were drawn back to her slim figure. Her pale face held a flush of excitement, he noted, like a kid on her birthday. She looked ridiculously small and slight to be a large-animal vet. The sooner she realized, it the better, or she was bound to get herself hurt. One big confrontation with a boisterous young bullock and she'd be scuttling out of here as fast as possible—or on her way to the hospital. She would probably do okay in the city, tending dogs and cats and fussing around their owners.

Even as the thought came into his head, guilt pricked his conscience. To be fair, Cass had proven herself as a vet so far. She just looked so...vulnerable. Her delicate features and huge dark eyes owed nothing to makeup, though. Whatever she had that drew him to her—and he had to admit she did have something—it was all natural. Not that she was his "type," of course. Tara's face slid mercilessly into his mind. Was *she* his type, then? Either way, he didn't intend to have a type ever again.

When the auctioneer's voice broke through his reverie, raised high above the crowd's babble and the horses' piercing whinnies, Jake walked over to Ray Johnston, who was trying to get a halter on one of his ponies.

"Want a hand with that?" he asked.

Ray looked around in surprise, then broke into a grin. "Yeah, thanks."

"You've met her before then, eh?"

"Who?" Ray asked as he slid the white rope over the pony's fluffy ears. He tied the rope to the rails and stood back. "Oh, you mean the vet?"

"Pretty small to be a horse vet, don't you think?" Jake remarked. "A gust of wind could blow her away."

"Oh, I don't know. What she lacks in brawn she more than makes up for in skill.

Came out to an injured pony of mine, to help Todd, and she had it calmed in no time. The lass has a way with her, if you ask me. Are you buying today?"

Relieved at the sudden change of topic, Jake was, for once, happy to reply. "There're a couple of interesting youngsters…depends on how much they go for."

"I have a couple of grand Fell ponies here if you're interested," Ray said.

"They're nice." Jake gave the ponies a cursory glance. "But I'm not really looking for natives. Something with a bit more blood suits me better. Good luck with them."

"Thanks again for the help," Ray called as Jake moved away into the crowd.

CASS HAD PARKED herself against the railing, determined not to miss anything. She leaned forward as a bedraggled Thoroughbred cross charged into the ring. Eyes bulging, it surveyed the mass of people beyond the barrier, letting out a screaming whinny.

"Lovely three-year-old, this," cried the auctioneer, raising his hammer. "By the Thoroughbred stallion High Star out of a hunter mare, it's sure to go a long way in the right hands. Now, who will start me at fifteen hundred?"

"Eight hundred," came a voice from up above her. Cass twisted around to see a raised hand in the first row of seats. Its owner was ruddy-faced and huge. She turned back to the horse, empathizing with its fear. It looked so…classy, she supposed, standing stock-still, neck arched and nostrils flaring. It deserved to go to someone who understood its sensitivity; you could develop a real bond with a horse like that. Her fingers tingled. But what would she do with an unbroken three-year-old gelding.

"Any advance on eight hundred?" the auctioneer shouted.

A murmur ran through the crowd. He raised his hammer higher.

"Going once…"

"Eight-fifty."

The auctioneer's eyes lit up as the bidding began to rise. Nine hundred, nine-fifty…. A battle between two people that surely had to end soon.

"Fifteen hundred," cut in a third voice.

Silence fell as all eyes swiveled toward

the new bidder. Cass peered through the crowd, but met a sea of blank faces.

"Going once," cried the auctioneer.

She saw the ruddy-cheeked man lower his eyes and knew he was out of the race.

"Going twice…" The hammer came down with a thud. "Sold…to…."

A clerk whispered in the auctioneer's ear as the high-strung horse pranced from the ring.

After watching a few more ponies—mostly half-wild yearlings—go through, Cass decided to wander around. She wondered who had bought the three-year-old bay, and found herself searching for it in the crowded pens. The same moment she saw its elegant head, raised above all the others, she spotted Jake. Then a cry rose above the babble of voices.

"Mind your backs!"

The bystanders pressed against the rails as a black shape hurtled through the crowd. A couple of burly dealers tried to stop the crazed Fell pony. Acting on impulse, Cass stepped forward, grabbing the rail behind her and sliding the bolt. As the pony came toward her, she opened the gate. It barged into the metal bars, knocking her backward, but the impact was enough to slow its flight. Cass clung to the cold metal, head reeling, and a tall man in a tweed jacket prodded the pony with a stick.

Suddenly the animal was safely back in its pen, and the man was smiling down at her as she raised her hand to her throbbing head.

"Well done," he said. "Brave move, that. Are you all right, lass?"

Cass nodded, trying to smile, feeling the stickiness of blood in her dark hair.

"I'm fine," she mumbled, and he turned away in relief as a firm hand gripped her shoulder.

"What were you trying to do, kill yourself?" The male voice that accompanied the hand was thunderously angry and somehow familiar, although everything seemed fuzzy and distant.

"Come on," he insisted, easing her up and almost carrying her between the auction pens and into the fresh air outside. Cass blinked, disconcerted to see Jake Munro's angry blue eyes staring down at her.

"What did you think you were doing?"

Her head cleared a little. "It would have hurt someone."

"Yes. You, as it happens."

Blood trickled down her forehead. She raised her hand, but Jake brushed it aside, dabbing her brow with a tissue.

"That was a crazy thing to do," he said, with slightly less anger in his tone. "You'd better go to the First Aid station."

"No!" She tried to pull herself together, shaking her head to clear it. "Honestly, I'm fine. I'll sit for a few minutes to be sure."

"Well, I can't leave you here."

"I'll sit in my car."

"No. Look, I have something to do, but my truck is just over there."

Within minutes, Cass found herself in the small living area of Jake Munro's surprisingly tidy horse box. She collapsed onto the seat, trying to keep control of her spinning head as he glanced out the window.

"Just go," she insisted. "I'll be fine."

Suddenly, the whole situation felt surreal. She was here, at a horse sale, with a man who didn't like her, and he was the only one helping her out.

"Thanks," she called after his retreating figure.

It was clear to Cass that he was in a bad place. His wife leaving, followed by the loss of his daughter and mother in one fell swoop—not to mention his son— had pushed Jake to the limit. It must have been—must still be—hard to get on with life after that much tragedy. But perhaps he had always been bad-tempered and unsociable.

Suddenly, he looked back with a concerned expression on his face, stretching his lips into something that was almost a smile. Maybe he did have a softer side, she thought. Or maybe the bang on her head was just making her delusional.

CASS WAITED IN Jake's truck for what seemed like an age. She'd slept, or at least she thought she had, but everything seemed a bit vague. The ramp at the back of the vehicle hitting the floor brought things back into perspective. *Was that the sound of unshod hooves?*

She stood up shakily, feeling a little odd but much less distanced from the world, and clambered awkwardly down the steps to see Jake trying to load a bay horse into the truck. Was it really the three-year-old she had seen in the sale ring? Jake glanced at her with no trace of his earlier smile remaining.

"Oh, you're still here," he said bluntly.

Cass felt a flicker of anger. "Sorry, I thought you told me to stay for a while."

"Oh, yes…" He lowered his gaze. "Are you okay now?"

She squared her shoulders, wanting to walk away but unable to resist asking about the horse.

"I'm fine. Is that the three-year-old by High Star? I saw him go through the ring."

Jake looked at her in surprise. "Yes."

"Shall I chase him up the ramp for you?"

"Well…" She could tell he wanted to refuse her offer, but common sense prevailed. "Thanks."

With Jake at the front and Cass's determined efforts behind, the nervous youngster was soon safely loaded.

"I'll be off then," Jake said. "Best get him home as soon as possible."

For a second, Cass held his gaze.

"Thanks for your help," she said quietly.

He narrowed his eyes. "Maybe you won't be quite so impulsive next time, eh?"

"Oh, I think I will," she responded.

The ghost of a smile brightened his clouded features.

"I don't doubt that," he said. "But you're probably concussed. Perhaps I'd better drive you home in your car. I know plenty of people here who'll take my truck back."

Cass shrugged. "I don't want to put you out, but…"

"Decision taken then," he said. "Meet me back here in half an hour."

CHAPTER TEN

CASS PULLED HER fluffy dressing gown closely around her as she waited for the kettle to boil. It had been a heck of a day, there was no doubt about that. While she was waiting for Jake, she'd gone back to the sales ring to watch some more horses go through. Her head had ached so badly, however, that she'd gone back to his truck to sit down, feeling grateful for his offer to drive her home. She'd been a bit apprehensive about having to make small talk, but fortunately, she'd fallen asleep as soon as they set off, only waking when he parked her car outside the cottage.

"Nothing that a hot drink and an aspirin won't cure," she said out loud, pouring hot milk into a large, flowery mug and breathing in the sweet scent of chocolate before collapsing in front of the television. A game-show host was prattling on about nothing, all big smiles and ridiculously white teeth. She switched channels to see a gladiator standing above his victim, sword raised, and pressed the off button before he could strike.

Closing her eyes, Cass tried to relive her first moments at the sale, the excitement, fear and adrenaline that loaded the atmosphere. She had enjoyed helping Ray with his ponies, too; it had made her feel part of it all. And then, impulsive as usual, she had done something stupid and incited the wrath of Jake Munro yet again. He had seemed to soften, though, after she'd helped him load the gelding. Or had she just imagined it? And of course, he'd driven her home. Then again, she thought, rubbing her temples, he hadn't really had much choice.

A knock on the front door brought her sharply back to the present, and she jumped up, running a hand through her hair and smoothing her dressing gown. The knock came again and she hurried down the hallway, suddenly nervous.

"Yes…who is it?"

"Don't panic, it's just me."

Donald's familiar voice brought a rush of relief, and she slid the bolt, stepping back to let him in.

"I thought you must have gone to bed," he said. "Sorry to disturb you so late, but I was at Jake's and…"

"He told you I had a bump on the head."

Donald nodded, heading for the living room without waiting for an invite.

"Something like that. Now, since you're obviously fine, how about putting the kettle on?"

Cass hovered in the doorway. "I'll bet it wasn't his idea for you to check up on me."

"Well, not in so many words. He told me about the accident, though, and said you should have gotten checked out, so I suppose he must have guessed I'd call in. What is it with you two, anyway? I know you got off on the wrong foot, but that wasn't exactly your fault, was it, about Rosie, I mean."

Cass shrugged. "No, of course not. Apart from the fact that he's antisocial and downright rude, not to mention arrogant, I guess he doesn't like female vets."

Donald raised his eyebrows, hiding a

smile. "Or perhaps he's afraid of women in general," he suggested. "After the fiasco with Tara I think he believes that all women are totally self-centered, untrustworthy and best avoided."

"Well, he's not a very good judge of character then," Cass said. "Now, do you want tea or coffee?"

AFTER DONALD HAD LEFT, Cass flicked the TV back on, idly watching a wildlife program. It had been nice to see Donald, and comforting that he had shown some concern. She could be dead in her bed for all Jake Munro cared. A sudden memory of strong arms supporting her as her head spun in circles sent a shiver down her spine, belying the thought. He must have a heart hidden somewhere behind that tough facade. And he must have loved Tara once. Maybe he still did, and that was what had messed him up. It must be weird to have once been married to a famous singer. Anyway, one thing was for sure; she'd be better off steering clear of Jake Munro, and no matter what Todd thought, there was no way she would ever ask him to teach her to ride. Perhaps she'd see if she could find a riding school somewhere nearby.

MONDAY MORNING, CASS'S day off, dawned bright and sunny. Anticipation brought a strange fluttering sensation to her stomach, and suddenly she felt wide awake, even though she'd been up until late with yet another difficult calving. Remembering the farmer's relieved expression as a heifer calf slid from his prize Shorthorn cow, she smiled to herself. Maybe the farming community was finally beginning to take her skills seriously.

The fingers on her bedside clock clicked to seven, and she reached out to cut the alarm before it rang. Ten minutes later, dressed in jeans and a bright red T-shirt, she raced down the stairs and into the kitchen, stopping for a moment to revel in a beam of sunshine pouring through the window. It was a sign, she decided. She popped a slice of bread into her new toaster and flicked on the kettle before opening her laptop to begin her search for riding schools.

After half an hour of unsuccessful

searching, Cass felt a sliver of disappointment and closed her computer. Surely there had to be *somewhere* near here where she could learn to ride.

Just then, a sound from outside caught her attention, a low but distinctive whimper.

She stood, pushing back her chair.

"Hello?"

The sound came again, louder now, and she stepped across to open the door. Something warm pressed against her legs and she glanced down.

"Puddle!"

The pup squirmed on the ground, her whimpers erupting into squeals of delight. Cass bent down to pick her up, breathing in her puppy smell.

"What are you doing here all by yourself?" she said as another dog emerged from the trees behind the cottage.

"What do you think you're doing, Bess?" she called across to the black-and-tan collie. "Your baby's way too small to be going for walks."

Bess approached cautiously. Cass held out her hand and she sniffed it.

"Hey, girl," she crooned. "I won't hurt your pup."

Bess wagged her plumed tail, confidence rising, and Cass gently scratched her ears.

"Come on, I guess I'd better take you both home."

As they walked down the lane, Cass heard the rattle of a large vehicle approaching long before it rounded the corner. Clutching the pup in her arms and calling to Bess, she moved close to the hedge, her heart beating erratically. She really had to stop getting flustered every time she thought Jake Munro might be nearby. Why did he make her so uncomfortable? It wasn't her fault that tragedy had colored his life, so how did he always manage to make her feel like she was in the wrong?

To her relief it wasn't Jake who appeared through the windshield of the four-by-four, but Bill Munro.

He braked, wheels sliding on the grit.

"Going somewhere important?" she asked.

Bill smiled, straightening his tie as he peered from the window. "Is it so obvious?"

"Well, you haven't dressed up like that just to go shopping, and you are driving a bit fast."

Bill grimaced. "Sorry, about that. I'm off to see my bank manager, cap in hand, but I think it'll take more than a suit and tie to impress him. I want to get a business loan to do up those unused buildings at the end of the yard and make them into holiday rentals. Trouble is, bank managers don't seem to take you seriously anymore once you've hit sixty."

"Then why don't you get Jake involved? You could work on the project together," Cass suggested.

Bill laughed. "I can't see that happening, can you? Jake doesn't take much interest in anything nowadays—apart from his horses, that is. Anyway, what are you doing with Puddle?"

"What is *she* doing with *me,* you might ask. She turned up at the cottage with her mother in tow, so I'm taking them home."

Bill glanced at his watch.

"Well, Jake will be in the yard. Just give him a shout. And thanks."

"No problem." Cass smiled as Bill's vehicle began to roll forward. "Good luck with the bank manager."

His voice floated back to her through the open window. "I'll need more than luck, I'm afraid."

The yard at Sky View looked deserted when Cass walked through the gate. She placed Puddle on the ground, shut the gate carefully behind her and headed for the house with Bess at her heels. The pup gamboled behind them, stopping to sniff every interesting scent.

"Come on, girl," she called.

Puddle ignored her, trotting off in the direction of the barn.

"You need to learn a few manners." She laughed, scooping the wriggling creature into her arms.

When she turned back toward the house again, Jake had materialized in front of her. He stood, feet splayed and arms crossed.

"What are you doing?" he asked sharply.

Cass started to respond, but an unexpected breathlessness stilled the retort that sprang to her lips. She put Puddle down, feeling awkward.

"I know you like the pup," Jake went on. "But I think stealing her is going a bit far."

Anger prickled as Cass took in his sarcastic comment. Standing tall, she stared straight into his eyes. "Right, so next time I find her wandering, I'll just let her get on with it, shall I?"

"You could have given me a ring," he said.

"So what you're saying is that you don't want me hanging around your precious yard uninvited."

He shrugged, reaching down to pick up the pup. "Well, sometimes gates get left open…"

"Not by me." Cass turned on her heel. "And don't worry—I won't be trying to do you any more favors."

She was almost at the yard gate when she heard him call after her.

"The three-year-old is doing well."

"Pleased to hear it," she responded, without looking back.

"I know you weren't trying to steal Puddle."

Slowly she turned, meeting his gaze

across the distance. "But you *are* saying that you don't want me turning up here?"

"Well, no. It's just…"

"That you don't trust anybody," she finished for him.

He had the grace to look down at his scuffed leather boots. "Something like that."

For the sake of their professional relationship, if nothing else, Cass bit back a cutting remark and walked determinedly back toward Jake.

"I'm aware that we haven't exactly hit it off so far, but you could at least show me a little respect," she said. "I know you blame me for Rosie, but I just did what had to be done."

The flash of pain that darkened Jake's face made her suddenly regret mentioning the pony.

"I know that," he murmured. "And thanks for bringing Puddle back. She likes to follow her mum, if she gets half a chance, especially now that all her siblings have gone."

"Even the black pup?" Cass asked in surprise.

He nodded, avoiding eye contact. "Someone came for him last night. Anyway, I'm afraid I have a phone call to make…"

IRRITATED BY WHAT felt like a dismissal, Cass watched Jake walk away. He could do with a haircut, she decided, noting how his thick brown hair, streaked with gold from days spent in the sunshine, came right over his collar. As if he was aware of her scrutiny, he ran his long, tanned fingers through his curls.

"By the way," she called after him. "I won't forget to shut the gate."

He raised one hand.

"Make sure you don't."

"Don't bother saying thanks," she muttered under her breath. Next time the pup ended up at her house, he would have to come looking for it.

UNCOMFORTABLY AWARE OF Cass's gaze and determined not to give in to the temptation to look back at her, Jake reached the kitchen door, deposited Puddle inside and closed it firmly. For some reason, Cass always seemed to draw him out from the apathy he had so carefully wrapped around himself. The only other thing that affected his emotions was his horses, but that was in a good way. He couldn't quite understand why, but Cass reminded him of all the things he wanted to forget.

The memories made his chest ache. Tara's beautiful, almond-shaped eyes, filled with a love that had disappeared.... And the twins, perfect and so alike, one entity split into two. How had everything gone so wrong? Had it all been his fault, as Tara claimed?

Annoyed at Cass for the effect she had on him and annoyed at himself for giving in to it, he strode over to the stable, slid the bolt on Carlotta's door and stepped inside, appreciating the peaceful gloom. But the stable, for once, did not feel like a haven. The memories descended in a tumult, taking over. When Carlotta pushed her face against him—totally trusting, totally real—he breathed in her familiar smell, but he still couldn't stop the onslaught of yesterdays.

HE AND TARA had been so in love the day they got married. Or had they? Maybe it wasn't true love at all, not even back then. Throughout their brief, whirlwind romance, Jake had been overwhelmed by her looks and so proud that, of all the men who were after her, she had chosen him. After the twins were born, though, she'd changed. At least it seemed to him that she had—always complaining that she was bored, that he didn't pay her enough attention, that she needed a new challenge. Thinking back, he realized that there had been some truth in her accusations. He had been selfish in a way, absorbed in his show-jumping career. Perhaps the breakdown of their marriage had been just as much his fault as hers.

They had muddled on, though, even after the fights started. They'd worked on their relationship for the sake of the twins. And he'd truly believed that it was working... until she became besotted by success.

Tara had always been able to sing. She had a deep, moving voice that tore at the heartstrings. Before the competition, she had done little more than sing around the house. When Jake came home from the stables one evening to find her glowing with excitement about entering a singing contest, he had been genuinely happy for her. He hadn't minded when she told him she was taking the twins with her to London.

"I haven't seen my mum for ages," she'd insisted. "This trip will kill two birds with one stone, so to speak. She can come along to look after the kids when I audition at the London venue. She'd love to see us."

Little did he realize that their lives were about to be changed forever.

DESPITE HIS AND Tara's constant bickering and sleepless nights with the twins, he had missed them all desperately when they went off to London. The cottage they'd rented not far from the stables had seemed so quiet without the twins' gurgling cries and sweet, smiling faces. He felt as if a part of him had been torn away.

Tara had called, of course, but less and less as the competition progressed. Eventually, Jake had managed to find time to visit them all in London. Tara had barely been at home, but he had spent time with Lucy and Robbie and had sadly come to understand, from Tara's overprotective mother, just how unhappy Tara really was, living in the country.

When Tara was voted the winner, with all the acclaim it brought her, Jake had known their relationship was doomed. His wife was destined for stardom, and there was no place left in her life for him.

Jake slipped a head collar over Carlotta's neat gray ears and began the satisfying task of grooming her. He had far too much to do to stand around feeling sorry for himself. No one could change what had happened. His marriage had been doomed from the moment Tara went off to enter the competition.

Tara's decision to leave him had come as a shock, but it was the kids who had suffered. They were only toddlers, and they missed their mum.

Jake's hand dropped down, still holding the body brush. The twins had soon adapted to their new life, though, hadn't they? They loved his parents, and they'd thrived on the farm until...

The newly released emotion overtook him, and he pressed his forehead against Carlotta's neck, holding back tears.

When Tara came up with her grand announcement it had sent him reeling.

"I've made a decision," she'd told him. "You and I are over—we both knew that a long time ago. But we have to decide what to do about the kids and I…"

He would never forget the self-satisfied smile that had turned her beauty, in that moment, into something harsh and ugly.

"I need to do this," she continued. "To follow my dream and see how far it takes me."

His response had been immediate. "You're not taking the kids away."

"I have no intention of taking the twins." She had been so decisive, so sure of her actions…so selfish in her plans. "I want them to stay with you. I won't fight for custody, but I do expect to have the right to see them when I get settled. We can do it legally."

The first wave of pain had been dulled by the realization that she wanted him to keep the kids. Then anger had descended like a physical force. How could she leave her children?

And then she had gone…just like that.

Packed a suitcase, kissed the children, and walked away to her new life.

When he went home to visit his parents to work through his pain and confusion, his mother, all-knowing, had soon put the situation into perspective.

"Look," she told him. "You're hurting. That's only natural. You can't be married for over two years and not miss what you had together. Tara was always a bit wild— you knew that when you met her—and free spirits rarely stay in one place for long. Obviously she needed more in her life. You still have the twins—that's the main thing. Why don't you come back home and make a business here, with us. I can care for the children, and we have plenty of free stables...."

His dad had simply nodded. "Good idea. You've been away too long as it is. And you'd better get a good lawyer."

And that had been it, a simple solution to a broken life. But it had never really been a solution, Jake realized. It had seemed fine on the surface, but he hadn't really gone along with the plan, not properly. Instead, he'd thrown himself into his career and left his parents to take care of the children while waiting for...waiting for what? Had he somehow expected Tara to waltz back into his life one day, asking for forgiveness? Had he even wanted her to?

A bleak darkness descended, weighing him down with the guilt that never lessened. His mother and Lucy were gone for good, and it was his fault.

BILL MUNRO DROVE home from the bank with his sights firmly fixed on the future. He had expected to be shut down by the impossibly young bank manager, but to his surprise, Nick McAdam couldn't have been more helpful.

"You see, Gwennie," Bill said gleefully as he turned into the yard at Sky View. "I'm not too old for a new project after all."

A cloud of melancholy momentarily dulled his delight. If only Gwen was here to share this joy with him. Right after she died, he had taken up the habit of discussing everything with her, drawing comfort from the belief that she was watching over him. Now, with new goals ahead of him, he felt her loss so acutely, it was as if it she'd died only yesterday.

Bill sat in his vehicle for several minutes, taking stock of his life. He always tried to keep a bright outlook for Jake's sake. His son, after all, carried more than enough misery and guilt for the both of them.

"You don't blame him, though, do you Gwen?" Bill murmured, knowing it was true. His Gwen would never lay blame on their son, and she would have been heartbroken to see how he had changed. What Jake needed, he decided, clambering stiffly out of his Land Rover, was to move on with his life.

As he shut the yard gate, Bill saw Jake emerge from Carlotta's stable. Desperate to share his news about the loan, Bill strode eagerly toward him. The dark expression on Jake's face, however, made him think twice.

"They'll have good homes, you know," he said with a reassuring grin.

Jake froze. "What will?"

"The pups. I presume that's why you're so down? You know, with the last one going. Except for Puddle, of course."

Jake frowned. "I don't care about the pups."

Bill hesitated, about to skirt around Jake's hostility as usual. Suddenly, though, the time seemed right to take another tack. "Well, what else is it, then?" he asked. "You can't brood forever, son. One of these days you'll have to get on with living."

"I am living."

"What, you mean dragging yourself around with rarely a smile on your face is living? Bad things happen. Your mother would be turning in her grave if she could see how moody and bitter you've become. It wasn't your fault, son, and you need to come to terms with it."

For what seemed to Bill like the first time ever, Jake looked him full in the face, allowing his hard mask of anger to slip.

"You reckon?" he murmured.

Bill placed a firm hand on his son's arm.

"You have to. How else can you survive?"

Jake's face contorted, releasing a glimpse of the pain he tried to keep hidden.

"I guess in a way it *was* the pups going that got me down," he admitted, obviously fighting to retrieve his self-control. "And Rosie, of course. I try not to get attached to things, but…I suppose I just don't like change."

"Trouble with you, Jake, is that you've become afraid of caring for anything or anyone. You're scared of getting hurt again, that's all. You'll miss so much happiness living like that."

Bill felt a dull ache as he watched his son struggle to control his emotion.

"But what right do I have to be scared of getting hurt when I hurt Lucy and Mom so much?"

"Life hurt them, Jake, not you. Maybe it was just their time. To waste *your* life, now that would be a crime. I know your mother would agree with that."

When the trace of a smile flitted across Jake's face, Bill slapped him affectionately on the back, feeling he had finally made a breakthrough. For Jake to admit to the guilt that had been dragging him down must be a step toward healing.

"Come on, son," he said. "Let me tell you my good news over a coffee."

CHAPTER ELEVEN

CASS FINISHED WASHING the floor of her small kitchen and stood back, admiring the result of her efforts. There was something very satisfying about having your own place, she realized. She must try and get her parents over for a visit. Her mum would love the cottage, and it would be good for them to have a break for once. It had been six weeks since she'd last seen them—perhaps she should go home next time she had two days off in a row.

A sudden knock on the back door took her by surprise. She glanced at her watch. It was only eight-thirty in the morning—who would come calling at this time of day? She heard another short, decisive rap. She hurried to open the door and found Bill Munro standing outside, his hand suspended in midair.

"Ah," he said, lowering it. "You're in.

Sorry to bother you, but I was passing and..."

Cass stood back, ushering him inside. "You don't need to make excuses—you're welcome any time. I'm not at work until this afternoon." She motioned him to a chair at the tiny kitchen table and put on the kettle.

Bill reflected on his reason for calling in at Sky Cottage. It had been purely on impulse, really, born of his breakthrough with Jake yesterday, when they'd actually *talked* for what felt like the first time since....

He pulled off his cap, turning it in his hands. He had to at least try to clear the air between his son and his new tenant. The problem was, he wasn't sure how to go about it. They'd probably never be friends, he knew that, but it would be great if he could persuade them to get along a bit better.

"About that son of mine..." he began.

Cass hesitated, looking at him intently. "What about him?"

"Well..." Suddenly, Bill wished he hadn't started this conversation. "I just wanted to say..."

"Wanted to say what? That you're sorry for the way he behaves?"

"Well, yes. But he does have his reasons for being so…you know…"

"Standoffish?" Cass suggested.

"I suppose that is putting it kindly," he admitted.

"You suppose right. To be honest, I find him aggressive and often downright rude."

Bill felt a jab of disappointment. "That's a bit harsh."

"I'm sorry," she said, pouring two mugs of coffee. She placed one in front of him. "I know it's none of my business, but I do know a little of what you've both been through. You don't need to make excuses for him."

Bill shrugged.

"Okay, point taken and subject closed. It would be nice if you two could be friends, though."

"I wouldn't hold out much hope there," Cass said with a rueful smile. "Although, I must admit he showed a slightly softer side when I hit my head, and Todd and Donald both seem to get on with him. I'd like to get more equine experience, and Todd even suggested I should ask Jake to teach me to ride. Fat chance of that. Unless…"

Cass tipped her head to one side, and Bill chuckled at her appealing smile.

"Of course, you could always suggest it to him—casually, you know, in passing—when you're both doing the dishes or something." Eyes sparkling, she lowered her voice into what Bill could only assume was an impression of him. "'Oh, and by the way, son, that new vet is looking for someone to teach her to ride. You could make a few quid there.'"

Bill's whole frame shook with laughter, and he reached into his pocket for a tissue. "I'll give it a go," he promised, mopping his eyes. "But…"

"You wouldn't hold out too much hope," she finished sadly.

"He hasn't always been this way," Bill insisted in his son's defense. "He used to have a sense of humor, just like you."

"I don't think I had much of a sense of humor before, either, until I came here," Cass said. "I think I was always very serious."

"That, my girl," Bill said, easing his aching bones, "is because you have finally found yourself."

Cass nodded.

"I was a bit homesick at first, but I love it here now. And I love my job, of course."

"You have to enjoy life while you can," Bill told her. "You never know what's around the next corner."

"I'm so sorry about your wife and granddaughter." Cass looked down at her hands, twisting her fingers together.

Bill remained silent for a moment, then he smiled. "Thanks. It's been tough. There will never be anyone like my Gwen, but we had a lot of good years. She loved having the children…"

"It's a shame you don't still have Lucy's brother. It might help Jake—I mean, to have him to care for…. Sorry, I know it has nothing to do with me."

"No…that's fine," Bill said. "You're only saying what I've been thinking for a year. Jake won't listen, though. It's as if he feels he should be punished, as if it's all his fault. Tara took Robbie away after the funeral, just whisked him off without asking."

"And hasn't Jake tried to get him back?"

"His lawyer is putting it through the courts. Jake has custody, you see. She has visiting rights, and of course she's his mother. Not to mention that she's very wealthy, which oils a few wheels. It's what's best for Robbie that counts, though."

"And what's best for Jake, too, surely. And you."

Bill stood up, draining his mug. "Thanks, but I don't think my son sees it like that. Anyway, I'd best be off. Sorry to burden you with my worries—I just thought it would be nice if you two got along. I hope you won't be too hard on him."

"I'll try not to be," Cass said. "By the way, how did you get on with the bank manager?"

Bill felt a spark of excitement. "Grand. He's given me the loan. Now all I have to do is…well, everything, I suppose."

"Don't give up on Jake," Cass urged. "Keep on trying to get him involved."

"And don't you give up on learning to ride," Bill said. "I haven't forgotten. Next time we're doing the dishes…"

"Maybe it should be when you're muck-ing out or something." Cass laughed. "I can't see Jake doing dishes."

AFTER BILL LEFT, Cass went about her household chores on automatic. The old man was right, she decided—she did feel as if she had finally found herself.

As she drove to work, she found herself looking forward to the challenges it held. Grumpy old farmers with aversions to female vets had become quite the norm, and she enjoyed gradually trying to get them all on her side. Bill's attempt to get *Jake* on her side, however... Now, that might be too much of a challenge. Jake had far too many issues, and he was definitely best avoided. She would find someone to teach her to ride, but it definitely wouldn't be him.

The surgery was already abuzz when she arrived. As well as the usual contingent of dogs, the patients today included a white rat and an African gray parrot.

"I think half the animals in the county must have fallen ill today," Todd grumbled as Cass walked into the office.

"Plenty to do, then." Cass laughed. "Do you want me in the clinic or out on call?"

Todd frowned. "You'd better go out on call. Don's had to go to the racing yard—suspected broken leg, I'm afraid. I can cover here. I'm waiting for a phone call anyway."

Perching his glasses on the end of his nose, Todd looked down at his scrawled notes.

"Mrs. Wilkes from Fell View Farm has a couple of calves with scour, so you'd better get over there first. Then Bob Macey has a heifer with an infected wound to see to, and there's a pony to check out farther up that road. Laminitis, it sounds like. Sally will fill you in on the details."

"I'm already on my way," Cass said, jangling her car keys.

As USUAL WHEN she was working, the shift seemed to fly by. Her last call was to Hill Close Cottage, where the laminitic pony was standing with its forefeet splayed, obviously in pain. She gave it a few shots to make it comfortable, then cautioned its young owner on the perils of overfeeding. Her phone buzzed just as she got in her car to leave.

"Hi, Cass, Sally here. I need you to go and see a horse at Sky View."

"Sky View," Cass echoed, her stomach churning.

"I know you've had issues with Jake Munro, but there's no one else. Todd is busy in the clinic, and Donald hasn't got back from the racing yard yet. Jake Munro will just have to..."

"Put up with me?" Cass said.

"Something like that," Sally agreed. "Or wait until later on."

"He may prefer to wait, but I'll give it a shot. Mr. Munro doesn't bother me."

If he doesn't bother me, then why is my heart beating so hard? she asked herself as she turned her car back up the hillside.

JAKE SAW CASS'S vehicle approach and cursed. Could he never get away from her? What was Todd thinking, sending her out here. He stood in Boris's stable, leaning over his half door, watching as she pulled up at the yard gate and climbed out. Her dark hair was loose around her shoulders, shimmering in the sunshine, framing her heart-shaped face.

"Hi!" she called with a broad smile, her dark eyes meeting his across the distance.

Something inside him stirred, and he took a breath, trying to turn the lurch of unexpected emotion into anger.

"Why hasn't Donald come?" he asked sharply.

Ignoring his question, Cass headed toward the stable and peered over the door.

"I presume this is the horse you called about?"

When she slid back the bolt, Jake placed his hand on the top of the door, holding it shut. "He's hard to manage," he insisted. "It would be better to wait for Donald."

"Look…"

Cass met his eyes with a steely determination, standing tall but still only reaching his shoulders.

"No one is available except me, so why don't you try to be civil and let me do my job—either that, or the poor animal is going to suffer until someone else can come out. At least let me look at the horse. If you don't agree with my diagnosis, you can wait for Donald."

Jake hesitated for a moment longer, unable to prevent a prickle of admiration from sneaking past his barriers.

"Okay," he said, stepping back. "Do your worst."

"Don't you mean best?" retorted Cass.

Jake gave a half smile, shaking his head. "I wasn't kidding, you know. He can be pretty mean. But if you want to try…"

"Just tell me what the problem is."

"I thought you were the vet."

She held his gaze unwaveringly. "Yes, and a vet usually gets some information about the symptoms from the person who called her out."

"Okay." He held up both palms. "Boris had an allergic reaction to something, so he needs an antihistamine shot. And I didn't actually call *you* out."

"That's hardly an outline of the symptoms—more of a diagnosis. No matter. I'll check him out for myself."

The big bay gelding shifted nervously from foot to foot as Cass approached. She murmured endearments while he sniffed her outstretched hand.

"Hey, big boy. There now, I'm here to help you."

Jake stood in the doorway, arms folded across his chest, observing her with amused interest.

"There's no way he'll let you treat him, you know," he told her. "He doesn't like women."

"And how do you know that?" Cass asked without altering her soothing tone. "There are no women around here to handle him."

Boris lowered his head, pushing against her, and Jake watched her place both palms around his huge cheek bones, moving them slowly upward to rub the backs of his ears. When the horse blew softly though his nostrils, accepting her, Jake's amusement faded into surprise. So she really did have a way with horses.

"When did they come up, the swellings?" she asked, gently outlining the raised lumps on the horse's neck and shoulders. "These are typical nettle rash lumps. His breathing is bad, too."

"For your information, I bought him from a woman. She was the one who told me Boris preferred men," Jake said. "And the lumps came up earlier this afternoon. So go on, what's your diagnosis?"

"You know exactly what's wrong with him. As you already pointed out, it's an allergic reaction, urticaria, and he needs an antihistamine jab."

"Better get on with it, then. Might not be so easy, though."

Cass turned toward him, looking him full in the face while moving slowly and quietly so as not to spook her patient.

"I've worked extremely hard to qualify as a vet, and believe it or not, I have actually administered shots to difficult horses before. So if I can get on with my work…"

Jake remained in the doorway as she approached, not giving her any other option than to squeeze past him. When her arm brushed against his, he froze, disconcerted by the warmth that passed between them. Her face was flushed. So she felt it, too. "Excuse me," she said, her voice soft and low.

He leaned down toward her, his lips close to her ear. "I'm sorry. I guess I haven't really given you a chance."

His heart pounded irrationally. What

was going on here? He didn't even like the woman. Their eyes met and held. "Thank you," she murmured "I'll get my bag."

Jake held the restless horse's lead rope, trying to attract his attention as Cass prepared to administer the shot. If he had expected her to seem nervous, he couldn't have been more wrong. She moved with a calm certainty that seemed to put the big horse at ease, running her fingers deftly across his silky coat and humming softly. It was done in an instant, with one smooth movement. Boris lifted his head, eyes momentarily wild as he felt the sharp prick. Cass rubbed his skin firmly, scratching his neck.

"There, boy," she said. "That wasn't so bad, was it?"

The rush of admiration took Jake completely by surprise. Cass turned back toward him, face bright with elation, and suddenly, somehow, she was in his arms, her body molded against him. Her lips were soft against his.

"No!" She pushed halfheartedly against his chest, cheeks burning, unconsciously raising her fingers to her lips as his eyes clung fiercely to hers.

It was he who broke away first.

"I need to see to Boris," he muttered, moving abruptly toward the big gelding.

CASS HURRIED OUTSIDE with her bag, crouching down to stuff her equipment back in and feeling totally unprofessional. What was she thinking? The few minutes before Jake reappeared seemed like a lifetime.

"Right then," he announced. His voice sounded too loud in the quiet of the yard. "He'll be fine now, so you can get going. And...sorry for...you know."

"What?" Her sharp reaction was instinctive. "Sorry for the kiss, or for not believing I could do the job?"

A glimmer of amusement brought unexpected warmth to his features. "For not believing you could do it, of course. I'm not sorry for the kiss. Don't worry, though, it isn't about to happen again anytime soon."

"That suits me," she said crossly, as Bill suddenly appeared around the corner of the stable block.

"Well!" The old man stopped in his

tracks. "You've actually allowed Cass here to treat Boris. Now that's a first."

Jake's eyes flicked back to catch hers, sliding away as she hid her confusion behind a forced smile.

"Yes, because he had no other option," she said. "And, unbelievably—according to your son—I managed to administer a shot without panicking."

"She did okay," Jake admitted. "Now I have chores to do, so perhaps you can take care of the tea-making, Dad."

Cass looked over her shoulder as she and Bill walked toward the cottage. Jake was standing quite still, his tall figure outlined in the sunlight, watching them. *This has got to stop now,* she thought, hurrying after Bill. This crazy love-hate thing between them had no place in her life. So why was the blood pounding so hard in her veins?

CHAPTER TWELVE

FEELING UNCOMFORTABLE ABOUT her kiss with Jake and apprehensive about seeing him again, Cass decided the best thing to do was to avoid him until she'd sorted out her thoughts.

As it happened, though, she didn't need to worry. The next couple of weeks were a whirlwind of work, with hardly any time for sleeping, let alone pondering that moment in Boris's stable. Donald was on holiday, leaving only her and Todd to cover all the shifts. One day ran relentlessly into the next, and even her dreams were filled with bad calvings and sick pets. The memory of Jake's lips on hers still simmered in the back of her mind when she was halfway between waking and sleeping, but during the day she managed to focus all her attention on work.

Her first afternoon off in nearly two

weeks found Cass stuffing laundry into the machine and trying to catch up on her neglected chores. As she turned on the washer, she heard a beseeching whimper from outside.

She recognized the sound at once—Puddle had escaped again. The breath caught in her throat, and Cass wished she'd never even seen Sky Cottage. There were far too many complications around here. Her fingers moved involuntarily to her lips, feeling once again the soft warmth of Jake's. Had he really kissed her, or had it all been in her imagination? She closed her eyes, remembering that moment of sweet tenderness. Oh, yes, he had definitely kissed her. She couldn't see him letting down his barriers like that again anytime soon, though. She would keep her distance from now on, she decided, putting Jake determinedly out of her mind. "Come on in, Puddle," she said, opening the door.

The pup bounded into the kitchen with an air of confidence, and Cass glanced around outside.

"What, no mum with you today?"

Puddle looked up at her, long tail wagging happily, and Cass reached down to pick her up. One thing was for sure— there was no way she was going to take the puppy back this time, or call Jake.

Cass dialed Bill's number.

"Hello, Jake here, can I take a message? I'm afraid my dad has left his phone at home again."

Cass froze.

"Hello?" Jake repeated.

"It's Puddle," she said. "She's over here."

Jake's voice held a hint of amusement. "And where might *here* be?"

Ignoring him, Cass floundered on. "You'd better come and get her. I wouldn't want to intrude on your privacy."

"Dad will be back in a minute. I'll send him. Oh, and…"

Her heart beat loudly in her ears.

"Thanks."

"You might try keeping a better eye on her."

Why had she said that?

When his phone clicked off, Cass let out a sigh. There was something about Jake Munro that brought out the worst in her.

Touching her lips again, she decided that was probably a good thing—she didn't want a man in her life at all right now, and certainly not one with Jake's issues.

Bill arrived twenty minutes later, full of apologies.

"You must think we're totally irresponsible," he said. "As soon as our backs are turned, Puddle just disappears."

"As long as she only comes over here, I guess it's not too bad. But if she ever got onto the main road…"

"Doesn't bear thinking about," Bill agreed. "Oh, and by the way, I asked him."

"Asked who what?"

"You know…not quite over the dishes, but…"

Cass's hand flew to her mouth.

"He didn't exactly refuse," Bill went on. "But let's just say I'm working on it."

The idea of ever being taught anything by Jake Munro brought a surge of panic.

"Don't worry about it," she insisted. "I wouldn't want to put him out. Please forget the whole thing."

"You wouldn't be putting him out," Bill

assured her. "Jake could do with a bit of female company for a change."

Cass shook her head. "Definitely not mine, I'm afraid."

The older man picked up the puppy, cradling her in the crook of his arm. "Don't be too sure about that. Thanks for rescuing Puddle again. We really will have to try and keep her locked inside."

Cass stroked the pup's head, and was surprised by the affection she felt.

"I used to have a dog," she heard herself say. "It was Bud who made me want to become a vet."

"What happened?" Bill asked quietly.

Cass felt tears prick her eyelids.

"He died. It was an accident—a car coming too quickly..."

"And his death made you decide to become a vet?"

She nodded slowly. "I could have saved him, you see...if I'd known what to do. It feels as if that's all I've focused on ever since—knowing the right thing to do."

"Well perhaps it's time you did get another dog, to lay some ghosts."

"It's nothing, of course, compared to what you've lost," Cass said.

For a moment, Bill just looked at her with a sad smile on his weathered face.

"When it comes to loss, there is no scale," he told her. "In a way, I suppose you and Jake are not dissimilar, both living in the shadow of lost love."

Cass frowned. "That's a strange thing to say…almost poetic."

"Ah, but very true if you think about it. You're both hiding behind lost love. The past is coloring your lives, and you need to move on."

"And you aren't hiding?"

"No, I hope not. Don't get me wrong, I have my black days, but my Gwen wouldn't want me to brood."

"I don't brood—at least not about Bud. His loss gave me my drive to be professional and to succeed. Thinking about him keeps me focused on what's important to me. Anyway, surely you should never forget your past. It's part of what makes you the person you are."

"Yes, of course it is," Bill agreed. "And you would never want to stop loving those you've lost. But you have to learn from your experiences and move forward. Remember the good times and don't dwell on the bad. Get on with living, and take all your memories along with you."

"Is that what you do?"

Bill was silent.

"I try to," he responded eventually. "But do you, Cass? You're obsessed with your career. Don't get me wrong—that's a good thing. You've given a bad experience a positive outcome, but perhaps it's time for you to move beyond that, to live a little more. Maybe even let love into your life. Work isn't everything, you know. Anyway, sorry for the lecture. I'd best be off. Thanks again for rescuing Puddle."

Cass smiled. "She's welcome here any time, and I don't mind the occasional lecture."

Cass showed Bill out, then sat down at the kitchen table, reflecting on his advice. He was right, of course. Even after the worst tragedy, somehow you had to pick yourself up and get on with living. Dwelling on what was gone was inevitable, though, to a degree. For her, dwelling had been a positive thing because she'd made herself a successful career from her experience with Bud. Despite what Bill said, her life was full. She didn't need anything more in it right now, especially the distraction of romance. Jake... Now, Jake was definitely living in the shadow of his tragedy, unable to recover. For a second, her hostility toward him evaporated as she saw the man through his father's eyes.

Feeling guilty and broken-hearted doesn't give him the right to be rude, though, does it? she reminded herself. Trying to understand Jake Munro was just too complicated.

FOR THE NEXT few days, Cass felt as if work was taking over her life, filling her every waking thought. When Todd announced at the end of a busy evening that Donald was returning the next day, and that she deserved a few days off, the determination that had propelled her through the past few days evaporated. All she wanted to do was collapse in her bed.

She retired early, just as the sun was beginning to sink behind the dark mass of the fell, but every time she closed her eyes, Bill's wise words came back to her. Relaxing her responsibilities, it seemed, had allowed the thoughts she'd been avoiding all week to emerge. Eventually, she gave up trying to sleep and went down the narrow stairs to make herself a warm drink.

The call came after she'd returned to bed and had finally begun to feel drowsy. She lurched awake at the loud, jarring ring, expecting to hear about an emergency at the surgery when she picked up the phone. Bill's urgent tone took her by surprise.

"Have you seen the pup?"

"No, but I'll go and check," she said, slipping into her dressing gown.

Outside, the moon was slowly rising and dark clouds chased each other across an eerie sky. She rushed back to the phone, internal alarm bells ringing.

"There's no sign of her, I'm afraid. How long has she been missing?"

"That's just it—we're not really sure. Some sheep were out, and I went up the fell with Bess right before dark. I shut Puddle in the house, but Jake came in soon after I left. She must have sneaked out then and tried to follow her mum. We hoped she was with you...."

"I'll come and help you look for her," offered Cass. "Give me five minutes."

"I'll pick you up."

Fear rose in Cass as she thought about the pup. She had really come to care for Puddle.

"Please let her be okay," she murmured, as she pulled on her clothes. Bill's Land Rover rattled to a halt outside, and she threw on her jacket.

As she clambered into the passenger seat, Bill flashed her a quick smile.

"I'm sorry about this, but there's a storm brewing, and the more pairs of eyes we have, the better our chances of finding her."

"Of course," Cass said. "Where's Jake, and what's the plan?"

Bill rammed the vehicle into first gear.

"He's gone ahead on the ATV with Bess to the area where I was earlier. The Land Rover won't make it up there, though, so we'll have to search on foot, I'm afraid. We don't really think the pup could have gone that far, but we've searched everywhere around the yard. I thought you and

I could do the lower slopes. Trouble is, if she's frightened, she could be hiding."

The thought of Puddle, lost and alone, made Cass's heart ache.

"Don't worry," she said with an outward show of a confidence she was far from feeling. "We'll find her, even if it takes all night."

A low rumble filled the darkening sky, and she glanced uneasily at Bill.

"'Course we will," he said.

When they arrived at the slopes, Cass breathed in the aromas of late summer—wet grass, wildflowers and the heavy scent of a nearby badger set. She clutched the small flashlight Bill had provided.

"You okay?" he asked. "Don't you go and get lost, as well."

"Don't worry about me," she responded, flashing her light around the undergrowth.

"Puddle… Here, Puddle… Where are you, girl?"

Slowly, Cass zig-zagged up the steep slope, calling softly. Now and then, bright eyes glowed in the beam of light and then disappeared. Her heart filled with fear.

How could a pup as young as Puddle survive in this hostile environment?

When lightning sparked across the sky, momentarily revealing the menacing hulk of the fell, despair flooded over her.

"Puddle," she cried again, her voice rising with the wind.

Thunder clapped overhead now, vibrating in her ears. She started to walk faster. The pup would be so afraid...or was she already home, wondering where everyone had gone?

Cass floundered up the steepening hillside, pushing through the bracken, panicking slightly when she realized she could no longer hear Bill in the distance.

"Bill!" she yelled. "Are you there?"

Thunder cracked again, and the desolate landscape was illuminated by a harsh bolt of light. When she was plunged back into darkness, her flashlight flickered off. She shook it, breathing a sigh of relief when it flashed back on again. She called for Bill again.

Something nudged Cass's leg, and time stood still. A scream rose in her throat but nothing came out. The nudge came again, urgent and real, accompanied by a familiar whine.

"Puddle!" Cass cried, falling to her knees.

The warm, excited creature that threw itself on her was a whole lot bigger than a puppy. She shone her light into shining brown eyes.

"Bess! Where's Jake?"

Waving her flashlight, she shouted his name, longing for the sight of his tall frame. When her calls were carried away with the howling wind, unanswered, she took a breath, wrapping her fingers into the dog's coat.

"At least we're not alone now, girl, but your pup is. Let's go find her." A faint mewling came from somewhere close by. Bess raced on ahead while Cass hurried after her, repeating the pup's name over and over. When a high-pitched squeal erupted up ahead, Cass came to a stop, trying to take stock of her surroundings.

"Bess? Bess, where are you?"

The squeal became a low moan just as a black storm cloud slid away from the silvery moon. A pale, ethereal light brought the world into vague focus, and she hurried up the slope, heart thumping as she followed the sound.

From somewhere below, a distant, excited whimper reached her ears, closely followed by a heart-rending howl of panic. Cass shone her fading flashlight into the underbrush.

"Puddle?"

In an endless moment, before another black cloud obliterated the moon, Cass saw the yawning drop ahead. Bess had gone over a cliff.

Throwing herself onto her stomach, Cass wriggled to the edge of the drop, peering into the darkness below. The dog's low moan floated up to her, followed by Puddle's keening cries. Hope returned. They were still alive.

"Hang on, girl, I'll save you," she cried. *But how?*

She had to get help—surely Jake was close by if Bess was here. Cass's voice was ripped away on the wind as she called his name again and again. When the dogs' groans continued, she knew she had to act now.

Remembering the cell phone in her pocket, she reached for it with relief. She could call Bill for help. Her numb fingers fumbled with the keys.

No signal. A sob stuck in her throat. There was no other option—she had to try and get down there. Bess was obviously hurt, but she hadn't fallen to the bottom. There had to be some kind of ledge....

With a final, hopeless yell for Jake, Cass pushed her flashlight deep into her pocket and swung her legs over the edge, straining for a foothold while clinging to the rocks.

"I'm coming, girls," she called to the frightened dogs below.

THE LEDGE WAS farther down than she thought. Her toes lost their hold, and for a moment she hung by her hands, convinced she was about to die. Images overwhelmed her. Bud's empty eyes... Puddle...

The puppy's high-pitched cries jarred her, and she searched inside herself for a last ounce of strength. Her fingers began to slip. Her feet fought for purchase, and suddenly they found it. Muscles burning, she slithered the last few feet, falling onto something solid. She was immediately greeted by a warm, wet tongue.

"Puddle!" Cass struggled to sit up on what felt like a very narrow shelf. She shone her flickering flashlight over the edge, cringing in fear as she realized just how vulnerable her position was. Stones showered onto the rocks far below as she wriggled around to look at Bess.

The sheepdog lay limp, whining under her breath. Cass carefully ran her hands across the dog's body, feeling the sticky mass of blood that oozed from a jagged tear across her ribcage. The grating bones in Bess's front leg told an obvious tale, but it was the bleeding that worried Cass most. Trying to stay calm, she searched her pockets for something to bind around the wound. She had to stop the bleeding…

"Hey, girl," she murmured. "You're okay now…"

Struggling out of her jacket, Cass pulled off her T-shirt, tearing it into strips for a makeshift bandage, oblivious to the howling wind as she wrapped the cloth firmly around Bess's body, trying to apply just enough pressure.

"There," she said when the task was complete. "Now let's check out that break."

The pale flashlight beam and Cass's capable fingers revealed a badly broken limb. Bess let out a cry as Cass tried to ease it into a better position. She needed to find a splint.

A bush, managing somehow to grow from the sheer cliff face, loomed out at her. If she could break off a branch.... Cass leaned over as far as she dared, trying to ignore the sound of stones crashing below. Thankfully, the branch snapped between her hands, and she tore again at her T-shirt, using her teeth to get another strip of cloth. She couldn't set the leg properly, but she had to make Bess as comfortable as possible until help came. Puddle was curled up in a ball, totally unhurt and happy now that her mum was there. Bess's eyes shone into Cass's through the darkness, and Cass felt suddenly helpless. They were all going to die, she was sure of it. If the ledge didn't collapse beneath their weight, then cold and shock could kill poor Bess. And what if they weren't found for days?

"Pull yourself together," she said out loud. She had to stay positive. "We are going to be okay."

She'd succeeded in helping Bess, and they were safe on the ledge—for now, at least. And Bill and Jake couldn't be *too* far away. Pressing herself against the rock face and trying to ignore the burning pain in her cramped body, Cass began to shout.

IT SEEMED LIKE hours before she heard the voices. Had she slept? Surely not. The sky was lighter, the storm had passed over and the wind had all but stopped. The voices came again, faint and distant, but very definite.

"Jake! Over here!"

Cass yelled until her throat was hoarse, until the words would no longer form. Bess yelped in pain as she tried to move. Desperately, Cass tried again.

"Here! Over here... Help!"

"Cass?"

Jake's voice was the best thing she'd heard in her life.

"We're down here."

His face appeared above her, peering at

her and the two dogs as they clung to the cliffside.

"Dad, quick! We need a rope."

"I'll take the ATV," Bill said.

"Hang in there, girls, you're going to be fine," Jake called down to them.

As the roar of Bill's engine faded and daylight crept over the skyline, Cass glanced around anxiously, realizing just how dangerous her predicament was.

"Stay still," Jake ordered. "We'll have you back up here in no time." His voice was firm, but the tone was gentle.

"Talk to me," she pleaded, needing reassurance.

The deep vibration of his voice echoed in her head as he rambled on, bringing a kind of peace as they waited for the sound of the ATV. Jake's words didn't matter— having him there made everything better.

"Thank you," she whispered as a faraway drone turned into a roar.

"Thank *you*," he told her, "You're doing great."

The emotion in his voice brought a warm rush of tears down Cass's face.

"Right," Bill said, his figure looming purposefully over the cliff top. "Let's get this rope down. Cass, if you can wrap it around Bess, we'll haul her up, then we'll drop it back down for you and the pup."

Fumbling in the pale dawn light, Cass secured the rope around Bess, praying it wouldn't make her injury worse.

"Got her!" Bill yelled from above, and Bess yelped as the rope began to lift her upward.

Suddenly, Cass's surroundings went blurry and she struggled to breathe.

"You okay, Cass?" Jake called.

The sound of his voice gave her new strength. She couldn't let herself faint, not now, when rescue was so close.

"Yes, I'm fine. Let down the rope."

As soon as Cass's head and shoulders cleared the cliff top, Jake hauled her onto firm ground while Bill grabbed Puddle from her. As much as Cass yearned to stay in Jake's arms, feeling safe, she pulled away groggily, turning her attention to Bess.

"We need to get her to the clinic. I think she's in shock."

"You two go," Bill urged. "Take the ATV, and I'll walk back down to the Land Rover."

CHAPTER THIRTEEN

CASS WOKE WITH a hammering in her head. She closed her eyes again as memories returned to her. Jake's arms around her as he pulled her to safety, the gentle timbre of his voice lending comfort.

She jerked herself fully awake. *Bess and Puddle.* Climbing out of bed, she glanced at the clock—it was almost eleven. What was she thinking, and what about work? A dull ache in her limbs made her wince as she pulled on some clothes and splashed water on her face.

It had taken half the night to treat Bess. Todd had met them at the clinic, but, despite Jake's insistence that she go home to rest, Cass had been determined to see it through. She'd helped Todd set the break, and she'd cleaned and stitched the dog's wound.

They had eventually left Bess at the surgery, recovering from her anaesthetic, and Jake had driven her home.

She needed to check on Bess, and she should have been at work already, she realized, hurrying down the stairs.

The phone was ringing when she reached the hallway. She answered it with shaking fingers.

"Cass," Todd said. "Are you okay?"

"Yes, of course. Look, I'm so sorry for being late. How's Bess?"

"The dog is doing fine. Jake just came by to pick her up. And don't you remember, I told you to take today off. You deserve it even more after last night. Some stunt you pulled, there."

"Anyone would have done the same."

"What, climbed straight down a cliff face you mean? I don't think so. As it happens, you did a great job. Both dogs could have died if you hadn't acted so quickly. You could have died, too, as a matter of fact. As your boss, I have to reprimand you. Health and Safety would definitely frown on your actions. As a friend, however, I must applaud you for your bravery."

"Thanks." Cass squirmed. "But it wasn't

bravery that made me do it. I have a habit of being a bit impulsive—acting first and thinking later."

"Ah, yes. I heard about your bump on the head at the horse sale. Anyway, I know Jake will be grateful. He does love those dogs."

"I didn't do it for him," Cass said. "Are you sure you don't need me today?""

"I gave you some time off, remember? And don't worry, I've got things covered. Now get some well-deserved rest."

"Thanks, Todd." Cass sighed, hanging up the phone. It was easy to act in a crisis, she thought. But now, remembering her fear, she was shaking all over.

HALF AN HOUR LATER, as Cass finished her breakfast, she heard a knock on the door. She realized she'd been waiting for it since the moment she woke up. She opened the door with a sense of inevitability, holding Jake's blue eyes with her own. His gaze was soft today, she noted, and bright like Bill's.

"I've come to say thanks," he said simply. "And to bring you a present."

"A present?"

"Yes."

He brought his arm around from behind his back, producing a wiggling ball of fluff.

"Puddle!" Cass said. "Is she all right?"

"Yes, thanks to you. And so is Bess. I've just taken her home."

He placed the puppy in Cass's arms, and she lowered her face into the thick coat, trying to hide her tears.

"Sorry, I'm…"

"You have a right to be a bit emotional," he told her, stepping inside.

"Todd said he had to reprimand me for not following Health and Safety procedures." Cass giggled, suddenly lightheaded.

"Thank God you didn't. Look, I just wanted to say…"

Cass looked up at him, aware of his discomfort.

"I want you to have Puddle."

"But she's yours. You wanted to keep her."

Jake stared at the ground, unable to meet her eyes.

"It's my way of saying thank you for

Bess. Todd said she'd have been dead if you hadn't acted so…"

"Rashly?" Cass finished.

"I was going to say bravely. Anyway, we'll only lose Puddle again, and she'll be happy with you."

A warm glow spread through Cass's body.

"But are you sure?"

Jake held her eyes with a calm certainty.

"I have never been so sure of anything in my whole life."

For an endless moment, she thought he was going to reach down and kiss her again, and she was vaguely disappointed when he stepped away. "Anyway…" he said. "Better get on. Oh, and…" He stopped in the doorway, turning back. "Maybe we will manage those riding lessons, eh?"

"I'd like that," Cass said, trying to decide if the emotion she felt was relief or regret. Definitely relief, she told herself as the door closed behind him.

To Cass's DELIGHT, Puddle settled in easily. She had expected the dog to pine for Bess, but by late afternoon it seemed as if Puddle had been there all her life. They had taken a trip to the shop to buy puppy food, a collar and leash, and a dog bed. Cass set the bed in the corner of her small living room, but Puddle immediately struggled up onto the sofa. With an exasperated sigh, Cass sat down, placing the little dog on her knee.

"We have to start as we mean to go on," she said in a firm tone. Puddle just licked her new mistress's fingers, totally oblivious to Cass's attempt at discipline.

Remembering the pup's recent ordeal, Cass sighed again, giving her a cuddle. "Well, just for now, then. After all, you're lucky to be here."

And so am I, Cass realized. She had been trying not to think about the almost-tragedy, but now the memories invaded, making her shiver. Some people might think she'd been brave, but she knew it wasn't true. To be brave you had to face your fears and rise above them—she never felt fear until after she had reacted.

Easing Puddle back onto the sofa, Cass reached for the phone, suddenly needing to hear her mother's familiar voice and already rehearsing a toned-down version of last night's events.

To her surprise and embarrassment, Cass was made to feel like a heroine when she arrived at work the next morning.

"Well, that's one way to get into Jake Munro's good books," Donald declared with a broad grin. He clapped her firmly on the back. "Seriously, Cass, well done. Bill told me about it. He said Bess would have been dead if you hadn't acted fast."

"Serious Health and Safety issues, mind," Todd remarked. "I'll bet you didn't do a risk assessment."

"Stuff Health and Safety," Donald said. "That's all this country ever thinks about. It's nice to see someone taking a risk for once."

The two men continued bantering as they left the office together.

"They never change," Sally said, smiling. "Now, I've made an area for the pup. It has a bed and toys and everything. I can keep an eye on her for you when you're working, since I'm always here at reception. I've run it by Todd and he doesn't mind."

Cass was choking up. Everyone was being so kind.

"Thanks for all the help," she murmured.

"No problem. It sounds like you deserve it. Did you really risk your life to save Bess and the pup?"

Thinking about clawing her way down the cliff face made Cass feel sick.

She shrugged. "They're all exaggerating. Anyway, I really appreciate your help with Puddle."

Sally scooped the pup into her arms.

"How could I resist?"

LIFE OVER THE next week or so slipped back into some kind of normality—as normal as it could be with Puddle permanently in tow—and Cass tried to put her memories of the night on the cliff out of her head. At least her experience had given her Puddle—it was all worth it for that. She tried not to think about Jake at all…until he called on Friday evening, just after the news.

Cass flicked off the TV and answered the phone, expecting to hear her mother's voice or someone from the surgery. Hearing Jake's deep tones, she snapped awake immediately.

"Puddle settling in okay?"

"Yes…yes, she's fine," Cass began, feeling like a stupid kid when her voice came out croaky. What was wrong with her? "Are you still sure you want me to keep her?"

"I don't give gifts to take them back again, you know."

She could tell he was smiling, and suddenly she was smiling, too.

"Well, she's the best gift I've ever had."

"Glad to hear it. Bess is recovering well, you'll be pleased to hear. Sulking a bit because she can't run around with the cast on, but she'll soon get over that. To be honest, though, the real reason I'm calling is to ask when you want to start those lessons."

"Bill put you up to this, didn't he?"

There was silence on the other end of the line. "Well…I guess he has been hinting. Says you deserve it."

"You don't have to teach me to ride, you know. Giving me Puddle is more than enough."

"No…" Did she hear awkwardness in his tone? "I want to," he insisted.

Cass felt a funny flutter of excitement in her throat.

"Then we can start whenever we're both free," she said.

"What about Saturday after lunch?"

"Great! I'm off this weekend."

Had she really made a date to have a riding lesson with Jake? she asked herself as he hung up. And did she really want one? Todd would be pleased, in any case, and learning more about handling horses would help with her career.

PUDDLE HAD ADJUSTED easily to her life with Cass and loved being at the clinic. On Saturday morning, she was waiting at the kitchen door when Cass came downstairs.

"Not today, girl," she told the eager little dog. "But you can come with me to see your mum later. You'll like that."

Puddle wagged her whole rear end, running around in circles, almost as if she understood.

Cass had been looking forward to her first riding lesson. She would have preferred it to be with someone other than Jake, someone she could distance herself from. The kiss still hung between them, never mentioned but oh-so-real. She worried that he'd returned to his grumpy self, or that she wouldn't meet his standards. Still, she was finally going to learn to ride, and he'd sounded quite friendly on the phone.

As lunchtime loomed, however, doubts set in again. She had bought herself jodhpurs and a riding hat, hoping they would make her look more professional. But when she studied herself in the mirror just before setting off for Sky View, she realized that perhaps she'd gone over the top…just like when she'd gone to Donald's. Jeans and a sweater would have done, she decided, wondering whether or not to get changed. She seemed to have a habit of wearing the wrong thing. Then again, the jodhpurs were a casual shade of blue, and they were comfortable.

With one last twirl, Cass called for Puddle and headed out the door. At least she'd made an effort. Why should she care about making a good impression on Jake, anyway?

THE LIGHT DRIZZLE that had been falling all morning slowly cleared as Cass walked to

Sky View Stables, allowing a glimpse of sunshine through the heavy bank of cloud. Cass felt her heart lift as she unlatched the gate. She really was going to learn to ride properly...at last.

"You made it, then?" Jake's loud voice boomed out at her from a nearby stable. He appeared in the doorway looking more jubilant than she had ever seen him.

"So you *can* smile," she remarked, moving toward him with Puddle at her heels. "Sure you haven't changed your mind?"

"Sure *you* haven't?"

She held his gaze for a moment, anticipation bringing a rush of heat to her face. Jake's face darkened, and he turned back into the tack room.

"Right then," he said. "We may as well get on with it. Follow me."

If Cass had expected to ride some kind of hairy, quiet cob, she was in for a big surprise. The horse Jake insisted she help him tack up was none other than the elegant, high-spirited Carlotta.

"You have to start out as you mean to go on," Jake told her, running an affectionate hand down the mare's arched neck. "If you want to be a horse vet, then don't just play at it—learn to handle a real horse."

Cass gulped back a response, trying to ignore the fluttering that made breathing difficult. He was right. If she couldn't handle Carlotta, then perhaps she should stick to dogs, cats and farm animals.

Jake proved to be a hard taskmaster. From the moment she bunched up the reins to mount, he demanded that everything be done correctly. She had to get on Carlotta's back from the stirrup, and as she strained to get enough bounce, she was suddenly glad of the jodhpurs—there was no way jeans would have stretched enough.

With a sense of satisfaction, Cass settled in the saddle for the fifth time, confident that she had mastered the mount. It was all about positioning and getting some spring, she realized, looking down at the top of Jake's head.

"Well, give her a pat," he said. "After everything she's just put up with, she deserves a bit of gratitude."

"Let's hope she's as long-suffering when we start to move." Cass smiled, leaning forward to give the mare a gentle caress.

Cass noticed Jake's eyes lingering on her fingers, then he turned abruptly.

"Right. Now nudge her with both calves and walk toward me."

Cass did as she was told, reveling in the sensation of the horse moving beneath her, taking her hips forward in a series of huge swings.

"I did ride a bit as a child," she said, her eyes alight with pleasure. "But that felt nothing like this. This is …"

"Like being part of the horse," Jake suggested.

"Exactly."

Their eyes met as they shared the moment, for once in total harmony.

"Now ask her to halt," he instructed. "And then walk on again."

WITHIN HALF AN HOUR, Cass was trotting around the arena with a huge smile on her face.

"You must have more riding experience than you're letting on," Jake said, impressed by her progress.

"Just trekking when I was young, and the occasional ride on a school friend's pony.

No proper lessons. I can't believe how at one I feel with Carlotta."

"Well maybe there *is* hope for you, after all."

"So you'll give me another lesson?"

"Hmm…" Leaning back against the fence, Jake made a quizzical face, looking down at Bess, who was observing the proceedings from right behind him. "We'll have to think about that, won't we girl?" he said, his tone serious. Bess wagged her plumed tail, and Jake broke into a grin. "Okay, I guess you're worth another shot," he told Cass. "How does tomorrow sound?"

"Shall I come up early and help out first?" she asked. "It's the least I can do."

Jake hesitated, panic suffocating him. He had let himself forget, and it felt so wrong.

"Sorry, I forgot… I have to go somewhere tomorrow. What about next week? Same time, same place."

"Thanks, that would be great," Cass said, sliding to the ground.

Jake stepped over to support her, holding out his hands then immediately drawing them back, trying to mask his awkwardness by making excuses. "You don't need my help. You've got to learn to do it by yourself. And don't think you're getting away with me doing all the work today," he said, smiling as he regained his composure. "You rode her, so you can untack her and put her away. She'll need a good grooming."

Their eyes locked in a rare easy moment.

"I'd love to," she said. "But you'll have to point me in the right direction."

CHAPTER FOURTEEN

CASS WAS LOOKING forward to her next lesson. She had bumped into Jake a couple of times over the last week, in the village shop and on a brief visit to Sky View to treat one of Bill's sheep. Jake had been distant and brusque, making no reference to her last riding session or even the one to come, but she refused to be daunted, determined to turn up at the time they'd agreed on and hope he remembered.

It was drizzling when she set off for Sky View, but she refused to let the weather diminish her enthusiasm. To her relief, Jake was already in Carlotta's stable when she arrived.

"I thought it might be too wet for you," he remarked, his blue eyes narrowed.

She held his gaze, smiling brightly.

"Do I seem like the kind of girl who's bothered by the weather?"

He shrugged, pursing his lips.

"You obviously don't know me very well," Cass said. "I'll just bring Puddle into the house, then I'll show you how *not* bothered I am."

The lesson felt as if it followed directly from their previous one, except that Cass had digested all the advice Jake had given her and had also read a book on the subject, improving her understanding tenfold. After several circuits of the sand school under Jake's stern scrutiny, she reined in, glowing with delight.

"It's even better than the first time," she exclaimed.

"Well don't stop yet," Jake said. "You said you didn't mind the rain."

Cass looked into his eyes, detecting softness and even a hint of admiration.

"Am I doing well?" she couldn't help asking.

"You are," he said with a rare smile. "Despite the rain."

Cass urged Carlotta forward. "Today I love the rain," she told him. "But come on, give me some advice. How's my position?"

JAKE HESITATED. THERE was something so heart-rending about Cass's obvious joy, and her face, pink with exertion and damp with the rain....

"You could relax your legs a bit more and try to loosen through your shoulders to keep your hands still. Every part of your body has to be under control, which isn't easy when you're trying to balance on a big horse like Carlotta."

Cass frowned thoughtfully, angling the mare toward him. "Show me," she said. "Then I can see how it should be done."

Jake paused again before taking hold of the mare's rein. "Okay, jump off, then."

This time he did put out a hand to steady her as she slid to the ground. Her body felt warm to his touch despite the rain. He snatched his hand back as if it had been scorched. What was he doing?

"Stand back," he said brusquely, vaulting neatly into the saddle. "I want you to watch how my hips go with the movement. They should be able to shift without affecting your shoulders or arms. You can't expect to control a horse if you can't control your own body."

CASS WATCHED, MESMERIZED, as Carlotta
floated around the sand school, gliding effortlessly sideways before breaking into a
rhythmic canter. They moved as one entity,
in total harmony.

"Do you think I'll ever be able to do
that?" Cass asked, hands on her hips.

Bringing the big mare to a halt in front
of her, Jake smiled—an open, easy smile
that held real warmth.

"Of course you will, if you listen to me.
Now get back on and try harder."

As they returned to the stable thirty minutes later, Cass couldn't stop talking, reflecting on her performance and asking a
string of questions, hardly taking in the answers before moving on to the next.

"If you don't slow down a bit, your head
might explode," Jake remarked. "There's
only so much information you can take in
at once, you know." Jake caught her eye,
and she noticed a glint of amusement.

She flushed, slightly embarrassed by her
own excitement.

"Sorry, I just enjoyed it so much."

"It's okay to be enthusiastic," he told her,
thinking just how long it had been since

he'd felt enthusiastic about anything. Silence fell between them, with only the squelching of eight feet on the soggy ground to break it. When they reached the stable he handed Cass the reins.

"I'm afraid I'm not always the best company," he admitted.

She shook her head. "I know you have your reasons, and I'm sorry."

He scowled, turning away.

"Don't be. Oh, and make sure you give the mare a good grooming. Brushes are in the box."

CASS REFLECTED ON that conversation a couple of weeks later as she took Carlotta into her stable after a lesson. That had been the first time she had actually felt a real connection with Jake, however brief it might have been—apart, of course, from their kiss. She tried not to think about the madness of that kiss. *And since then… Since then,* what? she asked herself, unbuckling the mare's throat latch and slipping the bridle over her ears, allowing the bit to drop gently from between her teeth. Since then, they had arrived at a kind of unspoken truce, she supposed.

Cass put on Carlotta's head collar, kissing her velvety nose before reaching for the grooming box. She was becoming quite adept at tacking and untacking, not to mention grooming and all the other horsey jobs she'd been practicing.

As she got to work with a body brush and curry comb, her mind still kept returning to Jake. Since that second lesson, they seemed to have developed a quiet camaraderie through their shared love of horses, their uneasy relationship replaced by something that was almost the beginning of a friendship.

They spoke easily now after the lessons, sometimes over a coffee in the farmhouse kitchen, about riding and horses and Cass's progress. They avoided anything even remotely suggesting emotion, and skirted around the memory of that kiss. Perhaps it was just she who needed to skirt around it—maybe it didn't rank high enough in his thoughts to need avoiding. She wished she could feel the same way...wished that the feel of his lips against hers didn't plague her dreams.

"There," she said eventually, patting Carlotta on the neck and putting her brushes back into the brand new grooming box she'd bought the week before. "We did well today, girl."

When a response came from behind her, she jumped, glancing around to see Bill's smiling face over the stable door.

"I agree," he said. "You're coming along in leaps and bounds. You're a natural, one might say."

"Thanks." She slipped off Carlotta's head collar and turned her loose. "I didn't even know you were watching."

"I've been following your progress these last few weeks, actually." His blue eyes twinkled. "I think Jake is surprised by how quickly you've come on."

"I just love it." Cass sighed. "He's a good teacher—that helps."

"It's nice to see him actually relax and enjoy something for once."

A warm glow spread through her. "Do you really believe that? Do you think he enjoys our lessons, too?"

"I know he does. I'm glad you've finally become friends."

Have we? thought Cass. *Friends—is that what we are?*

As she walked home, Cass thought about what Bill had said. Perhaps it was true that Jake enjoyed their lessons. After each one, she realized, he smiled a little more. And he talked more, too—except when he went into one of his black moods. Sometimes it seemed as if too much joviality made him turn inward, as if he was afraid of happiness. Or maybe he just couldn't let go of the sadness. Perhaps she should try and get him to open up, maybe even talk about the dark memories that colored his life. It helped to talk.

CASS WAS BACK at Sky View Stables for her next lesson a few days later. After negotiating her first jump over a small fence, she was on a total high.

"We need to celebrate," she said as she dismounted.

When she took a step back, losing her footing, she felt Jake against her. She froze, expecting him to back away quickly as usual. When he didn't, Cass's legs turned jelly. The moment lasted a lifetime.

"Celebrate how?"

His deep voice was next to her ear. She could feel his breath against her skin.

"Oh, I don't know. I just feel so…"

"Elated?" he suggested.

She twisted around to face him, heart thumping. His eyes burned into hers, and words evaded her.

"We could go out for a drink or something," she eventually managed.

How had she dared suggest that?

Suddenly, Jake's jawline tightened and panic flooded his face.

"No, I… No."

She pulled away from him, her face burning.

"Sorry, I'm just overreacting," she said. "It's a bad trait of mine, I'm afraid."

Jake seemed to have regained his composure. His eyes were narrowed now, his body tense. He was a million miles away from where he'd been only seconds earlier, yet there was still the vaguest hint of a smile in the curve of his lips.

"I've noticed that your bad…trait…does

play quite a big part in your life," he said. His expression hardened. "I knew someone else once who had that same trait."

Seeing an opportunity, Cass decided not to let it go. "And I'll guess that you loved her very much."

Pain flashed in his eyes. "Love is over-rated."

"Not when it's right…"

Suddenly he grabbed her shoulders, pulling her to him. "And has love ever been right for you?"

Cass stared into his eyes—they were dark with conflicting emotions. Now she wished she'd never pushed this conversation, never moved beyond the comfort zone of their almost-friendship.

"No, not yet. But I haven't met the right person."

He dropped his hands to his sides. "I thought I had."

Daring to take it a step further, she plunged on. "You still have your son. Surely a parent's love is unconditional—it can never fade"

Softness filled Jake's expression, smoothing out the harsh lines and bringing new brilliance to his eyes.

"You need to get him back, Jake. Bring him home where he belongs."

He turned abruptly, leading Carlotta away. "What if Robbie deserves more than I can give him?"

Cass felt dismissed. She had stepped over the line, she knew that, had gone beyond the invisible boundary they had set for themselves. Still, she dared to call after him. "I don't believe that, and you'll never know if you don't try to find out."

Was this the end? she wondered. Was their growing friendship—if it had ever been there at all—gone for good? Well, too bad. She had to say what was in her heart, had to try and make him face up to his emotions. Slowly, she headed for the house to pick up Puddle. She'd stay out of Jake's way for a while, she decided—give him a bit of space to sort out his feelings.

Cass was watching the pup chase her tail in the dusty lane when it hit her. She didn't want Jake Munro out of her life, even with all his problems. She wanted him in her life forever.

JAKE HEAVED THE saddle onto the rack, his head spinning. He had come to look forward to the time he spent with Cass. It had been easy, on his terms…until today. How dare she delve into his life like that. How dare she interfere. Anger rose, then seeped away when he remembered her warmth when she'd stepped back, almost into his arms. He had longed to twirl her around and kiss her like he had the last time. His desire was about so much more than physical attraction, though, and that was what scared him. He wanted to protect her, to hold her safe in his arms. That felt much too dangerous.

She'd wanted to celebrate—with him. Was that what had triggered this storm of emotions—the suggestion of a date? Or had she been asking him on a date at all? Perhaps it was all in his imagination. Then there was the stuff about love. What gave her the right to think she could hand out advice to him about his own son? She knew nothing about what had happened…about all the guilt and loss. She had no right.

Closing the tack room door behind him

Jake strode toward the house. Suddenly he felt so weary.

"You look a bit glum, son," Bill said as Jake walked into the kitchen.

Jake plunged his hands into a bowl of warm, soapy water in the sink, staring distantly out the window.

"I saw the lass leaving. Have you fallen out?"

Jake held his dripping hands aloft, considering his reply. "Kind of… I'm not sure."

He grabbed a towel from the hook and rubbed his hands dry, concentrating on the simple task. When Bill pointedly ignored his response, Jake glanced over to where he sat warming himself beside the stove. He suddenly felt the need to share his thoughts for what felt like the first time in forever.

"She asked me on a date," he said.

Bill raised his eyebrows. "And that's what you fell out over?"

"Well, no, not really. She said some other stuff…about Robbie."

"One thing you'll get with Cass is total honesty," Bill told him. "She won't skirt around the truth."

"I'm beginning to realize that."

"It's time to move on, son. Let go of the past and make a proper future."

Jake smiled. "You don't happen to have a bottle of sparkling wine around, do you?" he asked. "I think I need to build some bridges."

"And maybe knock down a few barriers," Bill suggested.

"Maybe," was all Jake could reply.

CASS HAD JUST stepped out of the shower when she heard a knock. She pulled on some clothes and ran down the stairs, still buttoning her blue checkered shirt as she opened the door. She saw Jake's tall figure and her heart flipped over. *So much for giving him some space*. He was probably here to tell her there would be no more riding lessons.

As she stepped back to let him in, she noticed the bottle clutched in his hand.

"You wanted to celebrate," he said, pushing the door shut behind him.

Cass stared at him. "But I thought..."

He was so close, she could feel the heat radiating from his skin. "You said..."

"I said a lot of things, and so did you. Most of them right."

She felt herself squirm. "Look, I'm sorry. I had no business telling you what to do with your life."

Jake shrugged. "But you couldn't help yourself, huh?"

"Something like that."

Reaching out his hand he ran a finger down her cheek. "Never stop being honest, Cass. Now go get some glasses while I attempt to open this bottle."

They sat awkwardly on Cass's small couch, like teenagers on a first date, sipping slowly from thick glass tumblers, unable to think of what to say. Bubbles burst in Cass's nose, and suddenly she was giggling.

"Who would ever have thought I'd be drinking champagne with Jake Munro?"

"It's not technically champagne," he remarked. "And I'm not an ogre, you know."

"But that's just it…" Her giggles subsided as her eyes met the intensity in his. "Sometimes it feels like you are."

Setting down his glass, he moved closer, placing an arm about her shoulders as if it was the most natural thing in the world. She rested her head against him, breathing in his scent of aftershave and raw masculinity. This felt so right.

"Then I'll just have to prove that I'm not," he murmured, his lips against her hair.

"I'd like that," she whispered.

For several minutes they sat together, unmoving.

"Do I seem like an ogre now?" he asked.

"Hmm."

She tilted up her face to look into his eyes, sniffing the air. "You smell okay. Aren't ogres supposed to stink?"

A smile relaxed his features. "It's been a very long time since I've followed my instincts like this, and I don't really know where it's going…or if it can go anywhere."

"Let's wait and see," she told him. "One day at a time."

"One day at a time," he echoed.

"And Jake?"

He drew back, looking down at her.

"Don't forget what's really important. Promise me you'll think about what I said…about Robbie?"

For a second his face clouded. "I already have. You're right—he is the most important thing in my life, and I'm going to get him back."

CASS SAT STILL for over an hour after Jake left, her mind buzzing, going through the day again and again. How could she have said those things to him? It had worked, though—that was the important thing. Jake was finally learning to live again.

What they had together was so new, so fragile, that they had to take it very slowly. Jake wanted his son back in his life; that was the priority. He was learning to let go, but was he learning to love again? As the thought jumped, unbidden, into her mind, she shivered.

He had started to allow her into his life—that was enough for now.

JAKE WALKED HOME SLOWLY. What had he started? he asked himself. He had enough problems without getting tangled up in a relationship. *Was that what this was?* The memory of Cass's warm body curling into his flashed into his mind and a sob tore at his chest. He didn't deserve happiness. It was Robbie who mattered now, and everything else had to take second place. Cass was right. He had to get his son back where he belonged—here at Sky View.

CHAPTER FIFTEEN

IT WAS ALMOST a week before Cass saw Jake
again, a whole week since he'd come to Sky
View Cottage with his bottle of sparkling
wine. He had been away at a sale for two
days, and she'd been working long hours
to cover for Todd, who had gone on holiday. She had plucked up the courage to
text Jake, though, a brief, cheerful message
about work and Puddle. He had texted her
back—she was pleased about that. Short
and impersonal comments they may have
been, like "waited all day to try to buy
a three-year-old but got out-bid," but at
least he was communicating. He even sent
a picture of a handsome bay in a pen with
the cutest pony she'd ever seen.

The texts held no hint of romance, but
perhaps that was for the best. Cass was
only too aware that this shift in their relationship wasn't going to be easy. Jake had

way too many problems, for one thing. Cass was just happy he had kept in contact.

She saw him as soon as she walked into the stable yard at Sky View, and her heart hit her boots when she noted his distant, aloof expression. Did he regret their moments of closeness?

"I've brushed Carlotta," he called. "Start tacking up and I'll be with you in a minute."

He entered the stable just as she was doing up the girth.

"I've followed your advice already," he told her.

Cass ran her hand under the leather to keep Carlotta's hair smooth, waiting for him to go on. Silence reigned, hollow and awkward.

"That's good," she managed eventually, sending him what she hoped was a cheerful, impersonal smile.

He cleared his throat. "I rang my lawyer for advice and he's getting back to me. I called Tara, too, half a dozen times. She didn't answer, but I left messages, so we'll see. Do you need a hand to mount?"

She shook her head, not trusting her

emotions, wondering where their newfound closeness had gone. Maybe he needed to focus on his son right now, she decided, walking Carlotta out into the sunshine. As she led the big gray mare toward the mounting block, Jake placed his hand on her shoulder, almost as if he were echoing her thoughts. She turned her cheek against the warmth of his fingers.

"I haven't forgotten, Cass," he said quietly. "I just need to take it one step at a time. Robbie has to be my priority before I...we..."

Looking up into his eyes, she nodded.

"I know that. It's important, for both of you. There's plenty of time for us."

He dropped his hand back down to his side. "Thanks for understanding."

DESPITE HER DISAPPOINTMENT, or perhaps because of it, Cass threw herself into her lesson, determined to do better than ever. Jake was distracted, she could see that, although they did share a moment when she moved on from negotiating simple crossed poles and jumped her first spread fence.

"I'll have to fork out for another bottle of

bubbly if you carry on like this," Jake said, putting the back pole up two more holes.

When they got back to the stables, however, he made his excuses.

"I've got to go," he told her. "You did great today, though."

"Thanks," she said, watching him walk off toward the house. For an endless second he looked back, meeting her gaze. When he raised his hand and disappeared around the corner, she sighed, turning her attention to Carlotta.

"Looks like it's just you and me now, girl," she murmured, pressing her cheek against the silken warmth of the horse's neck.

In a way, Cass thought as she set off for home half an hour later, she didn't mind taking things slowly with Jake. Puddle trotted at her heels, barking at a dragonfly, and Cass laughed out loud.

"I have enough on my plate with you, anyway," she told the pup, trying to convince herself.

The next two days were so hectic at work that Cass barely had time to think about

Jake, except in her dreams. She helped Donald foal a valuable Thoroughbred mare, dealt with an orphan foal and x-rayed a lame horse's hock.

Over lunch three days after her lesson, she opened up to Donald about her ambition to specialize in horses. He listened carefully, a thoughtful expression on his face.

"So basically what you're saying is that you're after my job?" he responded eventually.

Color flooded Cass's cheeks. "No, of course I'm not. I just..."

"I'm only joking. I think it's great to have ambition, and I'll help you in any way I can. How are you getting on with your riding lessons, anyway? Is Jake treating you okay?"

Cass paused, caught off guard.

Donald raised his eyebrows. "Is there something I should know?"

She was quick to respond. "Of course not. He's a good teacher."

"And...?"

"And nothing. Except that..."

"Come on. 'Except that' what?"

She felt herself brimming with excitement. "Well, don't say anything, but I think I've persuaded him that he really needs to get his son back."

"*You* have persuaded Jake Munro?"

"Don't look so surprised! I've had quite a few riding lessons now, and we've gotten to know each other a bit better, that's all. Well, enough to talk about things, anyway."

Donald's gaze held admiration. "Well, good on you, girl. He certainly needs someone to confide in."

"I can't say he confides in me, really," she admitted. "If I'm honest, I suppose I interfered—offered advice on a sudden impulse."

"Nothing new there." Donald smiled. "Sudden impulses do rather seem to be a specialty of yours. But hey, if you've gotten through to him, then well done."

AFTER HER SHIFT, Cass stopped off at the village shop on the way home. The door pinged as she pushed it open.

"Would you look at that," exclaimed Dora, the diminutive elderly owner of the busy little store.

"Look at what?" Cass asked, following Dora's gaze outside.

A low-slung, canary-yellow convertible slid across the square. Its glamorous, glossy-haired driver sported large, dark glasses. Beside her a small boy peered excitedly through the window.

Dora pushed past Cass and raced to the window.

"It's her," she said. "Tamara! You know, the singer."

Something tightened around Cass's heart. "You mean…"

Dora's lined face beamed. "That's right—Jake Munro's wife. Obviously, she's come back."

RETURNING TO SKY COTTAGE, Cass tried to put Tara out of her mind, but she couldn't bring herself to prepare a proper meal that night. Instead, she nibbled on a cheese sandwich, her head full of doubts. Why would Tara be here? If she'd come to bring Robbie home, something must have changed her mind. Or had she come back for good, come back for Jake? But why would she do that when she had the whole world at her feet?

Unable to resist the temptation, Cass headed toward the stables when she took Puddle out for her evening stroll. The pup, happy as always, followed behind her, sniffing at everything, while Cass walked slowly, her heart beating overtime.

The night was drawing in. Long shadows fell across the ground, and the leaves were turning a thousand glorious shades of red and orange. But for once Cass remained oblivious to nature's beauty as the stables came into view.

The yellow car was parked right outside the Munros' door, as if it belonged there—as if its owner had just pulled in to unload the shopping. *No.* She was being ridiculous. Tara had simply done as Jake had asked and brought Robbie home. *You should be happy for him,* Cass thought, *not worried for yourself.*

And *was* she worried? The answer came at once. Yes, she was worried. She and Jake had…something, but it could never withstand the history that he and the beautiful singer shared. Cass was supposed to be going for another riding lesson the next morning. Perhaps he'd ring and cancel now that Robbie was back.

"Come on, Puddle," she called. "Let's go home."

Jake's four-wheel drive was outside the cottage when she got back, parked erratically behind her car as if abandoned in a rush. He appeared suddenly, taking her by surprise.

"Cass…"

There was a ferocity in his eyes as he reached out to her.

"You don't need to tell me," she said, forcing an empty smile past a sudden sharp stab of jealousy. "I've already seen her."

"Seen who?"

Cass frowned. "Tara, of course. And Robbie. Don't tell me you didn't know they were coming."

Jake's face paled, and his hands fell to his sides.

"At my place?" he asked hollowly. "I'm just on my way back from town, and Dad is away for a couple of days. She never answered my messages."

"Well, it looks like she's here to do that

in person." Cass sighed. "You'd better go see them."

The heavy hand of doom settled over her as his vehicle roared off down the lane. Whatever happened now, it looked like their fragile new understanding was about to be put on hold. She had believed she was doing the right thing in encouraging Jake to fight for his son, but she hadn't considered the consequences for herself. Had she inadvertently thwarted their relationship before it had really begun? The little boy came first; there was no doubt in her mind about that. As for Jake… He needed to make peace with his past before he could move on, and having Robbie back was the first step.

JAKE DROVE TOO FAST, swerving into the yard and standing on the brakes. He saw the yellow car at once. It was so like Tara to drive such a vehicle. Hope swelled as he thought about Robbie. Had she really brought his son back to him?

Tara was in the kitchen, sitting at the table watching Robbie cuddle an ecstatic

Bess. He'd forgotten how the dog had always doted on the little boy.

She smiled at him, her beautiful face turned toward his as if he was just coming in from work on an ordinary day. He had the weirdest sense of déjà vu.

"Ah, there you are," Tara said.

"Dad!" Robbie shrieked, racing toward him. Then his son was finally in his arms again. Jake couldn't help the tears that flowed freely down his face—tears for Lucy, tears for his mum and tears for all the lost time without Robbie.

"Do I get a hug, too?" Tara asked, her voice honey-sweet.

Ignoring her, Jake buried his face in the little boy's hair, sweeping him off his feet.

"God, I've missed you, Rob," he murmured, glancing across to where Tara sat, elegantly draped across a kitchen chair.

"But as for you…" he began, anger lacing his tone.

Robbie stiffened. Tara caught Jake's eye, shaking her head in warning.

"As for me, what?" she asked brightly.

Jake changed his expression, forcing a lighter note into his words, his arm still around Robbie's narrow shoulders. "What have you been doing with yourself?"

"We've been having fun, haven't we, Robbie?"

The little boy scowled, hiding his blond curls against his father's sweater. "No."

"Yes, we have, Robbie," she insisted, staring at Jake defiantly. "We've been staying in the U.S. for the last few months."

"And that's good because…?" Jake cut in.

"It wasn't all work, you know. I took you to Disney World, didn't I, Rob?"

Robbie sneaked a quick look at his dad, the hint of a smile appearing.

"Yeah, and then later we went to see Harry Potter," he said.

"That's great, Robbie."

"I wish you'd been with us," Robbie added. "I went there for my birthday. I'm six now, you know."

Jake's chest tightened, and he searched inside himself for the apathy that had helped him survive the last year. It remained out of reach, revealing all the raw emotion he had tried so hard to overcome.

"I know, son," he said quietly. "Did you get my present?"

Robbie nodded. "Yes. Where's Gran?" he asked, looking around as if he expected her to walk through the front door.

For an endless moment, time seemed suspended as Jake stared into the innocence of his son's eyes. Could the boy really have forgotten, or was he unable to accept the loss?

"Gran's gone, Rob. You know that. She's gone to Heaven to look after Lucy."

"We talked about it on the way here, remember?" Tara said.

Robbie's pinched face turned even paler. "And where's Granddad?"

Jake rubbed his son's shoulders, glad to have some good news to relate.

"He's still here, he's just visiting his friend. I'll ring to tell him you're back, and I'm sure he'll rush home just as soon as he can. He's missed you, Rob. We both have,"

Robbie clung to his father's arm a minute longer, and then he smiled.

"Can I play outside until he comes home?"

"Not right now, Robbie, it's getting dark.

You can play outside first thing tomorrow, though. Your swing is still there, and your sandbox. You remember where they are?"

"'Course I do. But I'm too old for sand pits now."

Jake led Robbie to the staircase, not wanting to let the boy out of his sight but needing to speak with Tara privately and find out what was going on.

"You might be too old for sandboxes," Jake said. "But I'll bet you still like bikes. We can go get one tomorrow, too, if you like."

Robbie nodded eagerly.

"I've got a bike already, though."

"Well, you can have another one here."

The little boy's expression brightened. "Then I'll have two bikes."

"Only if you're good," Tara said sternly. "Now you go and play in your room for a bit while I talk to Daddy. All your toys are still there—I saw them when I took your suitcase up."

As soon as Robbie disappeared up the stairs, Jake's forced geniality with Tara slipped. He turned to face the woman he had once loved so much, feeling only anger and frustration.

"Why didn't you tell me you were coming? All the times I've tried to contact you, left messages, and you just turn up out of the blue."

Her perfectly made-up face contorted. "I brought Robbie here for his own good, Jake, not because you suddenly decided you wanted him back. He's found it hard to cope with Gwen and Lucy's deaths. I've had him in counseling, and they suggested that bringing him here for a bit might help him accept things."

"Maybe if you'd let him stay here after the accident, he'd be settled again by now. It was selfish, stealing him away like that."

"I can hardly steal my own son, can I?" Tara retorted. "I just thought it was best for him to stay with his mother—especially after you made such a botched job of looking after the pair of them."

"You seem to have forgotten something here…" Jake's voice was cold, his eyes as sharp as ice. "I am the one who has custody, and I am the one who calls the shots."

"That's not what my lawyer says…"

"I hate you both, and I want Gran!" Robbie stood in the doorway, yelling, hands over his ears and tears running down his face.

Jake was the first to reach for him, but in the split second it took him to cross the kitchen, Robbie turned and ran, disappearing into the darkness outside.

"You go find him this time!" Tara shouted. "He's been like this for months—running away every time someone raises their voice, crying in the night.... It's been hell."

Jake glared at her. What did she expect?

"We've made him like this," he said coldly. "And we have to fix it."

DETERMINED NOT TO allow her almost-but-not-quite relationship with Jake to affect her life, Cass was trying to keep herself busy, cleaning the kitchen floor until it gleamed with polish. She stood back, trying to ignore the questions that kept sliding into her head.

What did Tara want? Would Jake take one look at his ex and fall madly in love again? Cass tried to banish such thoughts, failing dismally. What did she care, anyway? She had her career—she didn't need a man messing up her plans. An image of Jake's face in the moment before she dropped her bombshell about Tara and Robbie popped into her mind. He had reached out toward her, his blue eyes filled with a fierce emotion. Now she'd never know what he was going to say. No matter, she told herself. She'd been fine on her own until now. Nothing had changed.

Calling to Puddle, Cass stepped out into the evening shadows. A brisk walk was what they both needed, she decided, to brush away those cobwebs. Or maybe she should leave them there to wrap around her heart—to protect it. She smiled at the thought.

"Cassandra Truman," she said out loud, "you must be going soft."

A sheep bleated loudly in the field across the lane, as though responding.

"You'd probably be better company than Jake Munro anyway," she told it, laughing.

Ignoring the temptation to head toward the stables, Cass took the pathway that led through a small copse to the edge of the property. Moonlight flickered through the branches above her, casting eerie patterns on the carpet of leaves beneath her feet. Puddle raced around in circles, excited by life.

"We've got each other, haven't we, girl," she said, stopping to absorb the scene. "What more do we need?"

Suddenly, a sound caught her attention—a kind of muffled sobbing. Was it human or was it an animal foraging in the undergrowth?

She hesitated, wondering whether to check it out or ignore it. When she heard another sob, louder and more obviously human, she moved slowly toward it, her heart pounding. If someone needed help, she couldn't just walk away.

Puddle found the child first. As Cass stepped into the clearing, trying to adjust her eyes to the darkness, the pup clambered into the arms of the little boy who sat huddled on a tree stump. He looked up at Cass through tear-filled eyes, and the breath caught in Cass's throat. She didn't need to ask his name. She hurried across the clearing and crouched down in front of him.

"She's called Puddle," she said. "And you must be Robbie."

He nodded slowly, showing no surprise that she knew his name.

"That's a funny name for a dog," he said, holding the pup close.

"I think you know her mum, Bess."

The little boy's blue eyes lit up. "My Bess?"

"Why, yes," Cass said, momentarily taken aback. "I suppose she is your Bess."

Puddle licked Robbie's face enthusiastically, and he smiled.

"Shall we go and find her?" Cass suggested.

Robbie placed the pup down gently, a puzzled expression on his face. "Aren't you going to ask me what's wrong, or why I'm here all by myself in the dark?"

Cass shrugged. "I guess you just needed some space. If you want to tell me why you're upset, then that's up to you, but it's your business. I want to help if I can, but I'm not going to pry."

The little boy absorbed her reply, frowning. "Where do you live?" he asked, taking hold of her hand. "Can we go there?"

Surprised by the emotion she felt at his display of trust, Cass pointed vaguely in the direction of the cottage. "I live over there, in your granddad's cottage."

"Do you know my dad?"

Cass paused. "Yes," she said. "I know your dad."

"And do you know my gran?"

In the brief silence that followed, Cass struggled for the right response. She shook her head sadly. "No, I haven't met your gran."

"That's because she's gone to Heaven to look after Lucy," he announced in a solemn tone, as if he was sharing a secret.

"Then what a kind person she must be," Cass remarked. "I wish I'd met her before she left."

"Maybe you'll see her when she comes back," he said brightly.

Cass just smiled, her heart going out to the confused little boy.

"I think I'd better take you home now. Your dad will be worried."

Robbie shook his head violently.

"He and my mum are fighting about me."

"That's hard."

"I wish we could all live together again. If Lucy and Gran come back, then me and Dad and Mum and Lucy and Gran and Granddad could all live at Sky View. There's loads of room."

"That might not be possible, Robbie, but you have all your memories of them, and you've still got your dad."

He nodded. "I've missed my dad."

Her hand tightened around his, and she drew him gently toward the pathway. He offered no resistance.

"We'd better hurry back and see him," she urged.

"Are you coming, too?"

"Not right now, but I'll see you soon."

"Promise?"

"I promise," Cass told him.

They could hear Jake calling as they stepped from the trees into the moonlit yard.

"Robbie… Robbie… Come on, son. It's okay." Jake's voice was raised in desperation.

Giving Robbie a gentle push, Cass whispered in the little boy's ear. "Go on then, go see your dad. He's not angry with you."

She slipped back into the cover of the trees as he raced off, her heart twisting as Jake held out his arms. Whatever happened between her and Jake, she realized, Robbie had to come first. He was confused enough without her interfering.

CHAPTER SIXTEEN

WHEN JAKE SAW Robbie's small figure appear from the shelter of the trees, the erratic thumping of his heart went into overdrive. He held out his arms as the boy ran toward him.

"Robbie! I was so worried," he cried, wrapping him in a bear hug. "I've been searching everywhere for you."

"Sorry, Dad. Are you angry with me?"

"No, of course not." Jake dropped to his knees, holding his son by the shoulders and looking into his tear-stained face. "I was afraid you'd get lost, that's all."

"Where's Mum?"

"She's waiting for you at the house. She's worried, too."

"She gets mad at me when I run off, but I don't care."

"Why do you run off, son?" Jake asked

gently, resting his arm across the boy's shoulders as they headed homeward.

Robbie shrugged. "I don't know… I just do. The lady helped me. She was nice."

Jake stiffened. "What lady?"

"The pretty lady with brown eyes—like chocolate. She said you'd be worried."

"And so I was. Where's the lady now?"

Robbie made a vague gesture. "She said she had to go, but I'm going to see her soon. She promised."

"Well, then I guess you will," Jake murmured, an image of Cass's face springing to mind. Chocolate eyes—it was a good description.

"Did you mean that her eyes are the color of chocolate?" he couldn't resist asking.

Robbie nodded. "Like dark chocolate, all warm and shiny. Your eyes are like the sky, and Mum's… Mum's change all the time. Gran's eyes are like chocolate, too, except hers are milk chocolate."

Noting Robbie's use of the word "are" Jake's stomach sank. The little boy still believed his gran was alive, still had to go through the grieving process. Was he in denial? One thing was for sure—Robbie had a hard road ahead of him. They all did.

"Come on, son," Jake said. "I'll race you to the house."

TARA WAS WAITING outside the front door when Jake and Robbie sprinted up to it.

"Robbie!" she snapped. "You have to stop doing this."

"It's okay," Jake said. "He isn't going to run away again—are you, Rob?"

The little boy shook his head. "Sorry, Mum."

"And you promise to play nicely while your dad and I have our chat?"

"I promise," he responded, already heading for his room.

JAKE STOOD BESIDE the stove, leaning against it as if he could draw comfort from its warmth.

"Right," he began.

"Right what?" asked Tara.

Jake studied her eyes, wondering what Robbie had meant when he said that they changed. Now they were a mottled green.

All of a sudden, Tara's attitude changed,

her hostility dropping away to reveal the charm that had first attracted him to her almost eight years ago. Her eyes turned almost amber as she stepped toward him.

"What do you want, Tara?"

"I already told you…"

She was so close now that he could feel her breath against his face.

"The counselor suggested that bringing Robbie back here for a little while might help sort him out. He won't accept that his gran and sister are dead, you see, and it's confusing him."

Jake moved sideways, uncomfortable with Tara's closeness. "So after everything that's happened you want us to pretend we like each other, for Robbie's sake?"

"Well…" She pursed her lips. "Is that so difficult? After all, as I remember, we liked each other quite a lot once."

"That was a lifetime ago—before you decided to abandon your husband and kids. You can stay in the guest room for a couple of days, while Robbie gets settled. He has his own room, of course. After that, you can go back to wherever you're living now, and leave my son where he belongs—here, with me."

"That will have to do, then…for now," she responded, smiling. "But he's my son, too."

Jake began to turn away, but she reached out with slender fingers and clasped his forearm, holding him back. "I'm not really as bad as you think, Jake," she said. "I'm just a young woman overcome by fame, I guess. I've actually been quite successful, as you might have noticed."

"I've noticed," he admitted. "But are you really able to care for Robbie properly, with everything else that's going on in your life?""

The scent of her perfume was heavy, clinging and exotic, unlike Cass's flowery fragrance. He pulled away from her.

"Two days is all I can do," he said. "And there's something you need to know—you'll never take Robbie away from me again,"

Tara's gaze was fathomless. She had always been pretty, but now, with her natural, exotic beauty enhanced by all that money could buy, she was stunning.

"I'm trying, Jake," she cried. "That's why I brought him back. But you're just as much at fault as me. We have to do what's best for Robbie now…whatever it takes."

Jake felt as if a trap was closing around him. Panic hit like a sledgehammer as he felt the truth in her words. She was right; he was just as much to blame for Robbie's state of mind as she was. The past rushed back to haunt him, a past that included Tara and the twins. He'd fought for so long to keep his memories and his emotions at bay, and now everything felt like it was hurtling out of control.

"Fine," he said, pushing past her. "Just a couple of days, though. After that, you have to leave."

BEING BACK AT Sky View, with all the memories it held, already seemed to be settling Robbie, Jake noted the next morning as the boy helped him muck out and feed the horses.

They hadn't heard a peep from him last night after Jake put him to bed. Jake had spent the rest of the evening in his office, uncomfortable with Tara's company and pretending to do some bookwork but achieving nothing. His mind had turned repeatedly to Cass. He just couldn't get her out of his head. Her slight, straight-backed figure mounted on the big gray mare, trying so hard to improve, and her face, angled toward him, bright and shining with genuine delight.

Tara had burst into the office, cutting off his train of thought, a mug of steaming liquid cupped between her hands. Placing it carefully on a coaster, she had perched on his desk.

"You can't keep avoiding me, you know," she had said. "We both need to make an effort to get along. Can't we at least try to act normal for the next two days?"

He had felt awkward, glowering at her like a school kid as anger swelled inside him. He'd tried to keep a lid on his feelings, but he'd failed.

"You blew any idea of normality away the day you walked out on me, Tara. I wouldn't have let you in the door if it wasn't for Robbie. I'll be civil, but that's it."

Remembering their conversation now, Jake sighed. What a mess it all was. He had a beautiful and very famous ex-wife staying with him, his son was a mess…and so was he, if he was honest with himself, looking back on the last twelve months. Even before that though, after Tara had abandoned them, he'd been wallowing in his own self-pity. He could see it clearly now, so why hadn't he seen it back then? He had opted out and left his poor parents to take care of everything. And now, when he had finally begun to believe that maybe, just maybe, he could move on, the past had shown up on his doorstep. This was a good thing, though, he reminded himself, his heart lurching with love as he watched Robbie. At least his son was back where he was supposed to be. She'd acted impulsively, but Tara had brought him home, and if that meant putting up with her for a few days, then so be it. It was what Robbie wanted that really mattered.

"Perhaps I could teach you to ride now that you're back," Jake suggested. It had always been Lucy who did the riding before—Robbie preferred books and watching TV.

The little boy grinned at the idea. "I could ride Rosie…until Lucy comes back."

Jake froze, unsure how to respond. "Lucy's not coming back, son," he said quietly, not wanting any lies between them. "And Rosie's gone, too, I'm afraid."

"Gone to see Lucy?"

"Yes…" Jake struggled for composure, very aware of the solemn eyes staring at him, waiting for answers. "I guess she has. But we can get you another pony, a gelding, maybe, that can be all yours."

Robbie thought about it, then nodded happily. "I can still get the bike, too?"

"You can still get the bike," Jake promised, wondering if spoiling the boy was the solution. "We'll go after lunch. Oh, and Granddad will be back today. He can't wait to see you."

"Will Gran be with him?"

"No, son. Look…" He dropped down to Robbie's level, taking hold of both his small hands and squeezing them. "You know that Gran won't be back, don't you? She's happy, though, where she is, and…"

"You're just like Mum," Robbie shouted. "My gran *is* coming back. I know she is. She has to."

A surge of emotion momentarily took away Jake's ability to respond. He stood, shoulders slumped, as the little boy glared up at him.

"Gran's with Lucy, Rob," he finally said. "In Heaven."

Suddenly, Robbie was running again, across the lane and out into the meadow. A hand gripped Jake's arm as he started to chase after him.

"Let him go, Jake." Tara's familiar voice was close to his ear. "He'll be back. He just needs to be by himself for a bit, and it's broad daylight now."

"He's only six years old," cried Jake. "I have to go after him."

"I told you he's been doing this since the funeral. It's why I took him to a counselor. It's safe here, and he knows his way around. The psychologists told me to give him space and let him come to terms with what happened in his own time."

"Fifteen minutes, then I'm going after him. He needs to know we care."

Tara smiled. "When did you become such an expert on kids?"

Jake shrugged. "Horses and kids, they have more in common than you'd think.

They need to know who's in charge and they need to feel safe and cared for."

"And when did you get to be so sensitive?" Tara asked. "What happened to the old Jake?"

He stiffened. "What do you mean?"

Her long, blond hair shimmered as she shook her head softly, green eyes glimmering. "If you'd been like this when we were together, maybe I would never have needed to go and find fame and fortune."

Jake's expression hardened. "That's ridiculous."

She raised her perfectly arched brows. "Are you sure about that?"

"I've never been more sure about anything. All you ever really cared about was yourself."

"That's not true," she said. "I never meant to hurt any of you."

"Didn't you?"

Seeing the cold, hard anger in his eyes, her face contorted. "Well, it was you who did the worst damage."

Jake turned his back to her and walked away.

"I'm going to find Robbie and take him

with me to pick up Dad from the station," he said over his shoulder.

"Jake…"

Something about the tone of her voice made him hesitate.

"I didn't mean that…and I'm sorry for… you know."

"I'll see you later," he said.

As he strode across the meadow to where he could see Robbie hiding in the long grass, he remembered Cass's lesson. He pulled his phone from his pocket and sent her a text.

Sorry, can't do today, will call and see you later, J.

"Robbie," he called. "Do you want to come and pick Granddad up from the train?"

The little boy didn't need asking twice.

"Now?" he yelled back, jumping to his feet.

"Right now. Come on, son. We'll bring Bess, too."

CHAPTER SEVENTEEN

"OKAY, THEN," DONALD ANNOUNCED. "Thanks for your assistance, Cass, but I think it's time you went home. You've been out half the night."

Cass gave their patient—a big bay mare with a nasty leg injury—an affectionate pat, then ran her hand through her hair, tucking it behind her ears before stretching both arms in the air.

"I guess you're right. I was called out around midnight and haven't been home since. I'm supposed to be riding at eleven-thirty."

"Not much time for sleep, then."

"It's only six-thirty. I can get three or four hours. Anyway, I won't sleep tonight if I stay in bed for too long. These nights really do mess up your internal clock."

Donald grimaced. "Tell me about it. My body clock stopped working years ago.

Enjoy your lesson, and I'll see you tomorrow."

Being busy for most of the night had kept
her emotions at bay, pushing thoughts of
Jake and his son to the back of her mind.
Now that she finally had time to herself,
though, her imagination ran wild.

She had never had much to do with kids
before, but Robbie had really gotten under
her skin the night before, and it wasn't just
because Jake was his dad. He had seemed
so vulnerable and confused.

Thinking about Robbie, she couldn't
help wondering how Jake was getting on
with his glamorous ex. It must be weird,
she thought, having someone as beautiful
and famous as Tamara staying with you,
even though they went way back. How
could any man resist her, let alone someone who shared so much history with her?
Hopefully she'd be gone by now.

Cass rounded the corner to see bright
morning sunshine bathing the cottage and
trees around it in a glorious golden glow.
She switched off her car engine and pulled
on the hand brake. It seemed strange to be
going to bed when the whole world was

alight with beauty. Perhaps she'd take Puddle for a quick stroll before climbing into bed.

"Come on, girl," she called, taking out her phone to check for messages. The screen was dark and dead, reminding her that she'd forgotten to charge it. She pushed it back into her pocket, making a mental note to plug it in as soon as she got inside.

By the time they had walked down the lane and back, Cass could hardly keep her eyes open. She ran upstairs and fell across the bed without bothering to get changed, waking up to the shrill ring of her alarm clock after what felt like five minutes. Puddle had grown used to the routine of the alarm, and she jumped onto the bed, licking Cass's face and putting all thoughts of closing her eyes again out of her head. Groaning, she sat up, tickling the pup's ears.

"Give me a break," she said. "You're only after food, anyway."

A few minutes later, she ran down the stairs, glancing at her watch. Ten-forty— she had twenty minutes to grab a coffee and get to the stables. The thought of seeing Jake, no matter what the circumstances, made her heart happy.

EVERYTHING SEEMED UNUSUALLY quiet when Cass arrived at Sky View. Even the horses didn't have their heads out over their doors. Cass found Carlotta pulling at her hay net. The gray mare nickered a welcome, looking for a treat, and she reached into her pocket for the carrot she'd brought, finding her cell phone instead. Shoot, she'd forgotten to charge it again. *Never mind,* Cass thought. She wouldn't hear from anyone at work, not after last night. Sometimes being on call was easy, but last night it had felt as if the whole world had problems.

Giving Carlotta a final pat, Cass headed toward the house to put Puddle in the kitchen before tacking up, half expecting to find Jake and Robbie there. How was he getting on with his son? she wondered. And was Tara still here? Noticing her yellow sports car, Cass's heart fell— obviously, she was.

When no one answered her knock, she slowly opened the back door, comfortable enough in her surroundings to know she didn't need permission. When Bess didn't appear to greet them, she frowned. Maybe she was outside somewhere with Jake. Cass decided she'd leave the pup here and go find them.

"Can I help you?"

The cool, high-pitched voice with its faint American twang took her by surprise. She stopped in her tracks, turning around to see Tara approaching.

"No, it's fine. I'm here for a riding lesson with Jake. I've just come to put the puppy here in the house. You must be Tara."

Huge, gold-flecked green eyes met hers, narrowing slightly.

"It's Tamara. And you are…?"

"Cass Truman. I'm…I'm a friend of Jake's."

"Oh, not just a client, then?"

Suddenly it felt important to Cass to stake her claim. "No, not *just* a client. I've known Jake for quite a while. Are you staying long?"

"That depends…" Tara drew herself up to full height, throwing back her shoulders and emphasizing her curves.

"Depends on what?" Cass asked

"On Jake. He and I are getting to know each other again, and of course there's Robbie to think about."

Ignoring her, Cass looked out the door, trying to slow the erratic thumping of her heart.

"He's expecting me," she said. "I have a lesson at eleven-thirty."

Tara stared at her a moment longer, then her full lips twisted into the semblance of a smile. "Don't tell me he's forgotten you were coming."

"No!"

Anger brought a hot rush of color to Cass's face. What right had this woman to speak down to her like that, insinuating that she wasn't important enough for Jake to remember? And what did she mean by "getting to know each other again?"

"Of course he hasn't forgotten. Where is he, anyway?"

"Well, that's just it." Tara didn't even try to disguise her gloating expression. "He's gone to collect Bill from the station, so I guess he did forget you, after all. He won't be home for a while, either, so there's not much point in hanging around."

As Cass crossed the yard with Puddle running along behind her, she could feel Tara's eyes burning into her back. It seemed that his ex wanted a whole lot more than to just drop Robbie off, whether Jake knew it yet or not. And how could he have forgotten their lesson, especially after... *After what?* Cass asked herself. What did they actually have? The hint of a relationship, the faint beginnings of love—was that what it was? She had told Tara that she and Jake were friends, and that was true enough. Was that all they would ever be now?

Trying to curb her anger, Cass quickened her steps, suppressing the urge to visit Carlotta again. Jake Munro was welcome to his beautiful, steely-eyed ex-wife, if that was what he really wanted.

"CAN YOU HEAR THAT, Robbie?" Jake said. They were standing on the train platform. "It'll be here in a minute."

Robbie jumped up and down. "I can't wait to see Granddad."

The train rumbled in, sliding to a halt beside them, and Jake closed his hand around Robbie's shoulder.

"You do want to stay here with me, don't you, son?" he couldn't help asking.

Robbie glanced up at him, eyes shining. "'Course I do, Dad. I want to live with you and Gran and Granddad again, like we used to do."

"And your mum?"

"Mum can stay, too…and Lucy, if she comes back. Look, there's Granddad now!"

Racing off down the platform, Robbie fell into Bill's outstretched arms. Jake's eyes met his dad's, recognizing his own emotion. *How do you convince a child that his grandmother and sister are gone for good?* If only Tara had left the boy here, where he belonged, then he'd have accepted the truth by now. Jake felt a stab of guilt. Maybe if he'd been a better father after Tara left, there would have been no reason for her to take Robbie away.…

Despite Jake's worries, Robbie's enthusiasm couldn't help but rub off on him. Bill's presence seemed to be having a good effect on the boy—Bill had a knack for asking all the right questions. They drove home on a high, and it wasn't until they were almost there that Robbie's insecurities returned.

"Will Gran be back soon, too?" he asked.

Jake caught his breath. He had meant to explain the situation to his dad on the phone, but the timing hadn't seemed right. Bill's eyes met his in the mirror, haunted by grief.

"I've told him she's got to stay in Heaven and look after Lucy," Jake cut in. "But he's still got you and me, haven't you, Rob?"

Robbie settled back in his seat, reflecting on his dad's words.

"She'll want to come and see Granddad, though," he eventually responded.

The two men were silent. Jake assumed his father was as aware as he was that they should say something to try and explain, but equally unable to put his emotions into words.

"We'll talk about it later, eh?" Bill suggested. "I see you've bonded with Bess again."

Robbie smiled, cuddling up against the dog on the back seat.

"I think she missed me," he said.

"I'm sure she has," Bill agreed.

Tara was in the kitchen when Robbie burst in, followed by Jake and Bill.

"Granddad's here," he cried.

Jake and Bill breathed in the unaccustomed aroma of cooking, glancing uncomfortably at each other.

"Hi, Bill. I thought you might be hungry," Tara said.

Bill refrained from comment, but sat down in the chair she ushered him to.

"I ate on the train," he said bluntly.

Robbie's face fell. "But I asked Mum to make a cottage pie because I knew it was your favorite."

Bill forced a smile. "Well, I guess I didn't eat too much, and I do love cottage pie. You have to have some, too, though."

"And you, Dad," Robbie insisted.

Jake sat down beside his father, feeling totally out of his depth. He'd dreamed about getting his son back, but he had no idea how to deal with this situation.

Oblivious to or simply ignoring the tension, Tara smiled.

"It's good to see you, Bill," she said.

Bill just nodded. "Thanks for the pie."

They ate in uncomfortable silence. Jake

kept making attempts at conversation, for Robbie's sake, but all his comments died before they left his lips.

"You'll be back off to the city tomorrow, I guess," Bill said to Tara. "Since you're only staying a couple of days."

"Home has been the U.S. for the last few months," she responded tersely. "I haven't got a base in London yet."

"So do you think you'll stay a bit longer, then?"

"Please say she can, Dad," begged Robbie.

Jake caught his father's eye, clearing his throat to buy time before answering.

It was Bill who spoke first.

"If it's what you want, Rob, I suppose she'll have to. Only another couple of nights, though."

The look of triumph Tara cast his way made Jake squirm

"I have to go out," he said, jumping to his feet. "I won't be long."

"And then can we go and get my bike?" Robbie asked eagerly.

"Then we can go and get your bike," he promised.

Jake walked quickly along the lane. He needed to see Cass, make sure she got his message and… *And what?* He thought he knew where he stood with her, but all these new complications made everything more difficult. Robbie had to be his first priority. He couldn't risk confusing the little boy any more, and Cass would understand that.

She answered his knock at once, as if she'd been waiting for it. He stood on the doorstep feeling awkward.

"Sorry," he said. "About the lesson."

Her expression was distant, strained.

"I had to take Robbie to the train station to pick up my dad."

"You might have let me know."

Robbie had said her eyes were like warm, dark chocolate, but there was nothing warm about them now.

"It was all a bit short notice. Didn't you get my text?"

A puzzled expression flitted across her face, and she rushed into the kitchen.

He followed slowly, feeling ill at ease, and found her flicking through her phone messages.

"It ran out of batteries," she said, looking up at him. "So you didn't just forget?"

He reached for her hand, closing his fingers firmly around hers.

"Of course not."

"I met Tara."

He grimaced. "And?"

"She's very beautiful."

"Yes," he agreed. "On the outside." Jake took her other hand, drawing her toward him. "I know it's a bit awkward, but Robbie seems really confused about his gran and his sister. It's as if he won't believe they're gone. I think he just wants his old life back. He's gotten to know his mum again in the last year, so I have to try and get along with her for his sake. You know that."

Remembering the little boy's sad smile and odd comments, Cass nodded. "I understand."

Should she tell him that she'd seen Robbie? she wondered, immediately deciding against it. This was between Jake and Tara, and she refused to play the part of the "other woman" and interfere. Jake had to sort it out as best he could.

"He's home now," she added. "That's what counts. Give him time."

Jake pulled her close, wrapping his arms around her and resting his chin on her head.

"You're right." He sighed. "It's just..."

She settled her head against the curve of his shoulder, not daring to meet his eyes.

"I know," she whispered.

CHAPTER EIGHTEEN

CASS FELT EMPTY after Jake left. She couldn't shake the sense that it was the last time he would ever hold her in his arms. Was their "almost" relationship already doomed?

The afternoon dragged. Cass wandered down to the village with Puddle, calling in at work on the way past.

"Can't you stay away?" Todd laughed. "You can do some overtime, if you'd like."

"Sure," she agreed. "Anytime. Oh, and is there any chance of a couple of days off in the next week or so? I need to go see my parents."

It had begun as a vague idea, but the stability of home suddenly seemed very appealing.

"I'll look at the schedule and let you know tomorrow," Todd said. "If you're serious about overtime, though, you can be on call again tonight if you'd like. Donald was supposed to be off this afternoon and on again later, but he's been called out to the racing yard at Doncaster. He could be hours."

Cass nodded happily. "That's fine. I have nothing else to do."

"Make sure your phone is on from seven-thirty then," he told her. "And give me a call if you have any problems."

Returning to the cottage, it dawned on Cass that Jake hadn't suggested another lesson. Did that mean he didn't want her around while Tara was there, or had he just forgotten? The reason didn't matter. She obviously wasn't welcome at Sky View right now, and that hurt.

"So WHAT COLOR do you want?" Jake asked Robbie as they drove to town.

"Red," Robbie said excitedly. "It has to be red."

"What color is your other bike?"

"That's red, too. It's my favorite color."

"And is that one in America?"

Robbie nodded. "JJ bought it for me."

"And who is JJ?"

"He used to be Mum's friend, but they don't like each other anymore."

"Did you like him?"

"He was okay. Is that the shop?"

Jake pulled over, sliding his big vehicle into a parking place. There was so much about his son he didn't know, he realized. "Come on," he said, taking hold of Robbie's hand. "Let's go choose."

The little boy's face lit up. "And then I can ride it?"

"Of course you can. I have to see to the horses, but if you help me muck out and feed them in the morning, then I'll come and watch you ride it for as long as you like. Deal?"

The little boy's grin said it all, giving Jake a warm, comfortable sensation. Sky View was already helping his son come to terms with things, he was sure of it.

On the drive home, Robbie pointed out the window as they passed the path that led to Sky Cottage.

"Does the lady with the chocolate eyes live down there?" Robbie asked thoughtfully.

Jake nodded, a hard lump forming in the middle of his rib cage. "Certainly does."

"Do you know her?"

"Yes…I do."

"She's kind."

Jake glanced back at him, meeting his serious gaze in the rearview mirror. "Yes, son, I guess she is."

CASS'S FIRST CALL came at seven-thirty. She picked up eagerly, glad to have something to focus on.

"Hi, Cass Truman here, what's the problem?"

The woman's voice on the end of the line sounded panic-stricken. "It's Sheba, my dog. She's having her pups, and I think there's something wrong."

Cass kept her response clipped and short, totally professional. "Okay, stay calm. Give me your address, and I'll be with you as soon as I can."

Running out to the car with her bag in hand and Puddle at her heels, she got inside and set the GPS. Yes, she decided, it was good to have something to focus on. She'd let her equestrian studies slip recently, too, so there was something else she needed to do. No more distractions—she would concentrate on her career from now on and let Jake Munro sort his own life out.

Helping the little terrier give birth to six pups wasn't the only job to take Cass's attention that night. Almost as soon as she got back to the cottage, her phone rang again. A farmer on the other end of the line insisted that she come at once.

"My daughter's pony has colic, and it's in a bad way."

The memory of Lucy's pony, Rosie, flashed into her mind and her stomach churned. That was the first time she had met Jake.

"I'll be right there," she said. "If you can tell me where you are…"

Cass eventually arrived home, tired but fulfilled, as the rosy light of dawn crept over the hills. To her relief, the colic had been treatable, and the little black mare was pain-free and comfortable when she left. It was nights like this that made her realize just how much she loved her job.

Puddle followed her, still full of energy,

as she climbed the the narrow cottage stairs for a well-deserved rest.

"It's all right for you," she said, smiling. "All you've done is sleep."

WAKING WITH THE SUN, Jake leaped out of bed, calling for Robbie.

"Come on, son, remember our deal."

The boy's bright face appeared around the doorway.

"Coming!"

"And don't forget to brush your teeth."

"I won't."

Robbie proved more skillful at handling a pitchfork than Jake remembered. He watched proudly as his son mucked out Carlotta's stable. He was so much bigger and stronger than when he'd last seen him. Jake felt a sudden ache for what he had missed. Children Robbie's age changed so much in a year, and he could never get that time back.

"Is that okay?" he asked, standing back to survey his handiwork.

Carlotta's bed was finished to perfection, the banks around the edges all neat and tidy. The mare sidled over and Jake patted her rump. "Okay girl, I'll let you go now," he told her, slipping off her head collar.

"Good job, son," declared Jake, wondering why he had taken so long to get the boy back when it was so obvious that this was where he belonged. "Only the feeding to do, and breakfast, then we'll give the bike a go."

Robbie's face glowed.

THE SMELL OF bacon met them when they entered the kitchen. Tara was at the stove, retrieving a tray from the oven.

"Right, boys," she said. "Who's for breakfast?"

Jake scowled, uncomfortable with the new side his ex-wife was portraying. What kind of game was she playing, and was it for his benefit, or Rob's? Maybe it wasn't an act at all; maybe she really had changed. Maybe fame and fortune hadn't turned out to be everything she'd hoped. *Not much chance of that!*

"I don't remember you making breakfast when we were married," he said sarcastically.

She stopped and turned to him, her face

pink and shiny with the heat. Suddenly, she looked once again like the girl he fell in love with.

"Thanks anyway," he said gruffly, sitting down. There was something very disconcerting about the way Tara was behaving.

When Bill came in, Robbie motioned for him to sit next to Jake

"Mum's made breakfast," he announced proudly.

"So she has," Bill responded as Tara placed a loaded plate in front of him. He smiled for Robbie's benefit and picked up his knife and fork, casting Jake an anxious glance.

"Anyway," Jake said, looking pointedly at Tara. "Shouldn't you be practicing or something? I thought singers had to do scales every day, to keep their voices in shape."

She turned away, busying herself at the sink.

"I'm not an opera singer, you know. I'm just taking some time off, that's all…to settle Robbie in."

"I'm riding my bike after this, Mum,"

Robbie said. "Will you and Granddad come and watch me?"

Relieved by the change in subject, Jake stood up.

"We'd better get on with it, then. I have horses to exercise later."

As Robbie wobbled around the yard on his new bike, Bill and Tara came out to watch, distracting the boy. His wobble turned into a tumble and he picked himself up, rubbing his knee as he tried again.

"I thought you could ride a bike," Jake called when he fell off for the third time in less than half an hour.

"He hasn't been on one for ages," explained Tara in the little boy's defense.

Jake frowned at her. "What six-year-old boy doesn't get to ride his bike?" he said. "Didn't your friend JJ help him?"

"He wasn't around that long. Anyway, there wasn't really anywhere to ride a bike in the city."

Jake glowered, suddenly angry. "Don't tell me—smart, expensive apartment with no backyard. Weren't there any parks? Maybe if you had fewer "friends," you'd have had more time for our son."

He regretted the comment as soon as it left his lips.

Tara's perfect features twisted into a frown. "Maybe if you'd been a better dad, he wouldn't have needed to be in the city," she yelled.

"And maybe if you'd been a bit less selfish, he'd—"

At that point, Bill stepped in.

"That's enough, you two. We're here to watch Robbie, not to fight."

Jake's face fell. What was he thinking, letting his pent-up anger at Tara out like this—in front of Robbie. He'd thought he was well past all that.

They turned simultaneously to see Robbie throwing his bike on the ground.

"I hate you," he screamed. "And don't you dare come after me."

"Don't worry," Tara insisted, holding Jake's arm to stop him from running after the little boy. "I already told you, he just needs some space. Bess is with him, so he's not on his own."

"I suppose that's his *counselor* speaking," Bill growled. "In my day, you used your instincts. You can see the boy is confused enough, and the last thing he needs is you two bickering. Maybe it's time you left, Tara."

Her face flushed and she threw back her shoulders.

"You told me I could stay a few more days," she objected. "Until Robbie's settled."

"He doesn't seem to be settling too well to me, whether you're here or not. And don't leave the lad on his own too long. You might think he wants space, but in my book it's love he's lacking…and stability."

"That's it," Jake said. "Dad's right. I'm going to look for him."

ROBBIE RAN WITH determination, trying to remember the way without having to follow the lane. He crashed through a small copse, blackberry bushes tearing his trousers. Disregarding them, he hurried on. Bess clung to his heels, not letting her young master out of her sight. Finally, Robbie came to a stop, taking hold of her collar for confidence.

"Here we are, girl," he announced, staring at Cass's cottage. Its small windows seemed to wink at him, welcoming him in.

CASS SAW THE boy through her bedroom window. He was standing with Bess in the cover of the trees. What could he want?

Running down the stairs, she stepped outside into the sunshine.

"Hello," she called. "Do you want to come in?"

Robbie didn't need asking twice. He bounded across the small garden and scooped up Puddle, who licked his face ecstatically.

"Come on," Cass said, taking his hand. "I'll get you a drink. Would you like a biscuit? You can tell me what you've been doing since we met."

Robbie said nothing. He sat at Cass's tiny kitchen table, tracing patterns on the brightly checkered tablecloth, nibbling on the gingersnap she'd given him.

She stood at the sink, washing the same few dishes again and again, wanting to appear normal, to put him at ease.

"Puddle was pleased to see you," she said.

The pup's whole body wriggled as she

wagged her tail, and Robbie smiled, reaching down to stroke her head.

"I was pleased to see her, too. Can I play with her?"

"Of course you can. You don't need to ask."

The little boy jumped off his chair and picked up one of Puddle's toys, a well-chewed fluffy rabbit, shaking it in her face. She grabbed it by the ears with her sharp little teeth and he burst out laughing, starting a game of tug-o-war. Bess oversaw the proceedings from nearby, as if watching over Robbie had taken precedence in her life.

"I think Bess likes having you back," remarked Cass, placing her tea towel over the bar of the stove and sitting down next to him.

"I've missed her," he said, looking up.

"And your dad, have you missed him, too?"

Robbie's face lit up. "Yeah. He bought me a bike, you know."

"Wow! What color?"

"Red and silver. I'll bring it to show you tomorrow, if you like."

"I'll be in after two-thirty," she told him. "But don't forget to tell your dad where you're going."

"And you don't mind me coming here?"

"You can come here any time. There's only me and Puddle. It's nice to have a friend."

The little boy turned his attention back to the pup, and Cass let him be. He could do with a friend, too, she realized, someone removed from the confusion of his young life.

"Do you think your dad will be worried that you're not at home?" she asked.

"Yes... I ran away."

"Does he know you're here?"

He shook his head, looking up at her with eyes so like Jake's they made her heart ache. She and Jake could have had something.... *Still could,* an inner voice whispered. *Or is it too late?*

"Can it be our secret?" Robbie asked. "Me coming here, I mean. Promise you won't say anything to Dad?"

"I promise, but you'd better go find him now, or else he'll come and find you."

Robbie nodded gravely and jumped to his feet, giving Puddle a final hug.

"I like secrets," he said. "Come on, Bess."

Cass curled up on a chair after Robbie left, the pup sleeping contentedly on her knee. She stroked Puddle's head absentmindedly, remembering Tara's caustic remarks. She was a woman about to fight for her man, Cass could see that, but why would Tara want him back now, after everything?

Robbie was their common bond, of course, so if Tara and Jake still had anything romantic left between them, then maybe the right thing for Cass to do was to back off and leave them to it. For the child's sake. Her every instinct, though, was to stand up for what she thought she and Jake could have, to try to stay in his life.

She thought of his scent as she'd pressed her face against his chest, the feel of his arms holding her, their growing closeness during her lessons, the humor they shared. It dawned on Cass just how far they had come. Their relationship wasn't all about romance or even falling in love.

She and Jake had been able to laugh together about little things, like Puddle's antics and the way Carlotta sometimes made a fool of Cass—one time, she'd fallen off the mare's back and ended up covered in mud. They'd become friends without her noticing, and even if it could never grow into a full-blown romance, she wasn't about to let that friendship go.

GUILT SUFFOCATED JAKE as he pushed through the bushes, trying to imagine where a confused little boy might decide to go to escape his dysfunctional parents and the conflicting memories Sky View held. He was only six years old, for crying out loud—he shouldn't be out here all alone, no matter how safe Tara thought it was. Jake didn't care what it took; from now on, he was going to make sure Robbie had the best childhood he could give him.

As his calls disappeared into nowhere, worry weighed him down. Tara had insisted they back off, that Robbie would return when he was ready. For Jake, that wasn't an option. He had deserted his son for far too long, wallowing in his own self-pity and guilt. It was time to make amends. Perhaps things would be better if Tara went back to the U.S.—no more fighting parents—but what if his mum's departure left the little boy even more insecure? Robbie had pleaded with him to let her stay, and Jake had the horrible feeling that the boy wanted them to get back together again, like a proper family. That was definitely not in the cards. His ex-wife might be beautiful and famous, but their love had died long ago—no matter how much she wanted to do for Robbie.

"Robbie!" he yelled again. "Robbie, where are you?"

Suddenly, there he was.

"I'm here, Dad. Sorry I ran away."

Jake felt his body deflate as a heavy sigh of relief shuddered through him. "That's okay, son. Let's go find Granddad and Mum. They're looking for you, too."

CHAPTER NINETEEN

TO CASS'S DELIGHT, Robbie was waiting for her when she arrived home from work. True to his word, he was proudly sitting on his shiny new bike.

She jumped out of the car with a broad smile on her face. "I hoped you'd come," she said.

His eyes were bright, she noted, full of laughter, and his face looked less drawn than the day before.

"I said I would. You wanted to see me ride it. I told Dad I'd be back home in half an hour, though, so I can't stay long."

Cass smiled at his eagerness, concerned that Jake didn't know she was spending time with Robbie, but not wanting to lose the little boy's trust.

"I'd love to see you ride it. Why don't you go along the lane and back."

The surface was rough, and despite Robbie's attempts to control the bike, she could see that it had a definite wobble.

"That's very good, Robbie," she told him. "I can ride a bike, too, you know. Would you like me to show you?"

He nodded, circling back toward her as she went to retrieve the elderly bike she'd found in the shed.

"You see," she called, glancing back at Robbie as she rolled down the lane. "The best thing to do is get a bit of speed up. The slower you go, the harder it is."

"Will you help me?" Robbie asked when she pulled up in front of him again. "I'm not very good at it. I keep falling off."

"I'd love to," Cass said, glad to help. "All you need, really, is a bit of practice."

FOR THE NEXT half hour, Cass watched Robbie riding up and down the lane, shouting directions. As his confidence grew, so did his ability to control the bike, and he eventually pulled up with a broad grin on his face.

"Do you think I've got better?"

"You know you have," she said. "You

should go home now, though, or our secret will be out."

"I'm going to ride back," he announced proudly.

"But didn't you ride here?"

He hesitated, a bashful expression on his face, then he grinned. "I pushed it," he admitted.

"Well," she said. "Now you won't need to."

It was surprising, Jake thought, as he watched his son riding around the yard a couple days later, just how much Robbie's cycling skills had improved in such a short time. It wasn't long since he'd run away after falling off it three times in thirty minutes, and now he was tearing around with newfound confidence.

Jake stood in the shadow of the oak tree, not wanting to distract his son. He so wanted him to settle in here and think of Sky View as home again, but apart from when he was riding his bike or helping with the horses, he still seemed very reserved for a six-year-old. It felt to Jake as if all his attempts to draw his son out of his shell just made the boy retreat from him even more.

He'd tried to talk to Robbie about Lucy and his gran, but he appeared to have blocked out all memories of those terrible days after the accident. Looking back now, Jake could understand why. If he was totally honest with himself, he had to admit this part of Robbie's trauma was mostly his fault. Unable to see past his own grief and guilt, Jake had left Robbie to Bill, who had been suffering, too. Tara had stolen him away before Robbie could even begin to come to terms with what had happened to his sister and gran. Jake wasn't sure he could ever forgive her for that, but now he saw the part he had played in his son's confusion. Tara wasn't all to blame, but Robbie was going to stay at Sky View, so perhaps it was time for her to leave and let Robbie readjust to life without her. He'd talk to her tonight, he decided, and just tell her that it was time to go.

Jake found his moment after Bill went to a meeting in the village and Robbie was tucked up in bed. Tara was watching a romantic movie on TV, painting her nails. The harsh aroma of nail polish triggered memories.

"You always used to do that," he said.

She glanced up at him, smiling.

"And you always used to moan about it. I usually have someone else do it now—someone else to do my nails and someone else to moan at me."

Jake felt an unexpected surge of interest in the life of the woman he'd once thought he knew so well.

"With all your success, I figured it would be you who called the shots."

She raised her eyebrows dramatically. "You must be joking. My manager is a tyrant."

"What's it like?" he asked. "Being famous?"

She shrugged, surveying her bright red nails. "Not all it's cracked up to be. You can't go anywhere without being recognized—in the city, at least—and Louis, my manager, is always on my back. To be honest…" Suddenly, her face crumpled. "I miss what we used to have, you and me. That's why I came back here with Rob. Don't worry, I don't expect you to fall in love with me again, but can't we at least pretend to be a family for a while? Just think of the stability it would give Robbie. I could do with a break, and after a couple of months I can start working again and gradually stay away for longer and longer..."

Her huge eyes were damp and misty. To Jake's annoyance, he felt the prickle of an emotion that wasn't anger.

"You can't actually be serious," he said as her words sank in.

"It wouldn't be for me," she insisted. "It would be for Rob. We owe him, Jake."

"Don't you mean *you* owe him? You started this, Tara."

"What do you mean?" Her tanned cheeks paled. "It was losing Lucy and his gran that traumatized him."

Silence fell between them. Then, in a low, fierce tone, Jake asked the question he hadn't been able to ask until now.

"Why did you do it, Tara? Why did you walk out on us like that...and then steal Robbie away..."

She hesitated, placing her polish carefully and deliberately on the table.

"What can I say?" she began. "I was young. You were never there." She turned to him, her eyes burning with emotion. "I had a chance, Jake, a chance to be *someone*. You were already someone, with your shows and your horses. The kids and I always came second."

"But I loved you and the twins," he cried.

"Not enough. You didn't love us enough." Her expression hardened. "If you're honest, you know things had already started to go wrong between us before I left."

He nodded slowly. "So you decided it was payback time, decided to go for it and leave *me* with all the responsibility for once. But why steal Robbie away like that?"

"You'd messed up, Jake. After I left, you just moved from our situation into a parallel life, expecting your parents to do what I used to. When I saw Robbie again, I couldn't bear to leave him behind. He didn't have his gran anymore, and Lucy was gone..."

Jake felt deflated, all the anger he had stored up for years sucked out of him. Wearily, he pulled himself to his feet.

"All this talk of pretending to be a family again is crazy, but you can stay for a little while longer. Then you have to go

for good, but Robbie…Robbie stays here…
permanently."

"Thanks," she murmured, looking down
to hide her smile.

CALLING TO BESS, Jake stepped out into the
yard. Darkness folded around him, soft and
all-concealing. Bess's cold nose nudged his
hand. The need to see Cass overwhelmed
him—the need to hold her slight shape
in his arms, to look into her warm, honest face. She would never walk out and
leave her children—he knew that with no
shadow of a doubt. With hope in his heart
squeezing through the mire of guilt, he
headed for her cottage. She was the only
good thing in his life at the moment…after
Robbie, of course.

He was doing it again, he realized, seeing
the situation totally from his own perspective. It didn't matter what he wanted—it
was his son who really counted. How could
he ever make it right with Robbie if he sent
his mother away and brought a new woman
into his young life?

Sky Cottage loomed, a dark, solitary
shape against the beam of a harvest moon.

A single light shone in the hallway, like a beacon, but Cass's car was gone. Maybe it was better this way. Maybe it was time to do the right thing for once. He would go and see her tomorrow, to explain that they needed to put their relationship on hold for a bit longer. Surely she'd understand. Car headlights broke through the velvety darkness. Were they hers? Should he stay a little longer and speak to her tonight? Temptation clawed at him. No…he needed to have his head on straight before he spoke to her, needed to think things through some more. As her car shuddered to a halt in the lane, he slipped away into the trees behind the cottage.

AFTER THE LAST few busy nights, Cass was relieved to have an evening off, and it had been good to catch up with Clare again. They had shared some Chinese take-out and a couple of glasses of wine, and their conversation had been light-hearted, touching on Cass's work and Clare's lack of a love life, but nothing more serious. She had left with a promise to repeat the visit next week. She found herself already looking forward to it, noting, not for the first time, that she spent far too many evenings alone.

Cass pushed her key into the lock and opened the door, holding it for Puddle to trot through, trying to decide whether or not to take a break from her studies tonight. She had spent most of yesterday afternoon filling her head with complicated information about horses. She had to get on with her career and her life, and she felt better for having a focus that had nothing to do with Jake Munro. Well, not directly, anyway.

Study had always been her bolster in life, she realized, as she reached for her new veterinary manual. Ever since she'd watched Bud die in her arms and decided to become a vet, when something went wrong in her life, she'd drowned her sorrows in books. Was that what life was all about? she wondered, a series of moments that forced you into decisions that could be life-changing? If Bud hadn't died like that, would she still have become a vet? If Puddle hadn't fallen down the cliff face would she and Jake still be angry strangers?

In a couple of days, Donald was taking her to see the stud in Newmarket, and she planned to read up on all the stallions there. Pushing Jake Munro to the back of her mind, Cass fed the pup, made herself a sandwich and settled down at her desk.

CASS HEARD BESS, scratching and whining outside. The sheepdog had visited often enough over the past few weeks for her to instantly recognize the sound. She hurried to open the door and froze when she saw Jake's tall shape in the darkness.

"Can I come in?" he asked.

She could tell from his voice that something serious had happened.

"Is everything all right?"

"I just need to talk to you, that's all. To be fair, I guess. Talking things through isn't one of my best skills, as I'm sure you've noticed."

Cass perched on the edge of a kitchen chair while Jake remained standing, appearing uncomfortable. A pulse beat in her throat, taking her breath.

"It's Robbie," he began.

"Is he okay?"

"Yes…well, if you can call it okay. He's

confused and insecure. Tara has been taking him to a counselor in the States—that's why she brought him home, to help him find some clarity."

Cass wanted to tell him she knew more about Robbie than he realized, but remembering the boy's face when he'd asked her to keep their friendship secret, she decided against it.

Suddenly, Jake smiled. "I know you met him that first day, when he ran away. He said he'd seen a lady with chocolate eyes."

"And is that a compliment?"

"Robbie seemed to think so. Anyway, thanks for looking out for him."

"He's a lovely little boy."

"I've messed up, Cass…"

Seeing the raw pain in his eyes, Cass's heart flipped over. "How?" she asked quietly.

He slumped down onto the chair beside her. "I let my kids down when they needed me, and if I'm totally honest, I let Tara down, too."

"But how can you say that when she walked out on her family?"

"I'm not forgiving her for it, I just hadn't

seen how selfish I've always been, until now. Everything has always been about me. My career, my hopes, my pain...and look where that got me. What I'm trying to say is..."

His head dropped into his hands, his shoulders hunched. Cass wanted to reach out to him, to run her fingers through his golden-brown curls, to hold him. Instead, she sat quite still, paralyzed, knowing what was coming next.

"What are you trying to say, Jake?"

He looked up, meeting her gaze. His jaw clenched and unclenched. "I care about you, Cass. A lot. But I have to put Robbie first. Tara is still here, and she wants to stay until Robbie feels more settled. How can I say no when it's what he wants, too?"

"And you want to put our...relationship on hold until she's left and he's in a better place."

He stared at his hands, twisting his fingers together. His palms were calloused, she noted with a rush of tenderness.

"Something like that," he admitted.

"But what about friendship, Jake? Surely we can still be friends?"

He reached out to take her hand. "If you'll settle for that...for now."

"So you'll keep up my lessons?"

Jake nodded. They stood simultaneously, eyes locked, fingers entwined.

"Robbie said your eyes were like warm, dark chocolate," he remarked.

"And do you think they are?"

He pulled her toward him, holding her for an endless moment.

"Oh, yes," he whispered against her ear. But it was he who pulled away first. "I'd better go."

She nodded, wondering how she would ever be able to see him as just a friend.

Cass didn't remember her lesson until he was walking off with Bess.

"When shall I come and ride, then?" she called after him.

He stopped, turning back. "Come tomorrow if you'd like. Midafternoon."

"I'll look forward to it. And Jake? I do understand, you know—about Rob."

Cass closed the door and sat down, going through their whole conversation again and again. What had Jake been trying to tell her? He'd said he needed to give Robbie the best chance he could to come to terms with the past and regain his confidence, but did that include giving his ex another chance, too? Instead of reading between the lines, Cass had jumped in feet first, talking about friendship and begging him to keep up with their lessons. She felt like a needy fool. He had asked for space and that was what he wanted.

All night she tossed and turned, falling asleep in the early hours and waking at dawn. By seven o'clock, she was out walking Puddle, breathing in the autumn air. By the time she got back to the cottage she had made her decision.

She stared at the phone, having second thoughts. Was this really the right thing to do? Before she could change her mind, she dialed the number for Sky View, her heart pounding.

"Sky View Stables, Tara Munro here. Can I help you?"

Cass felt herself tense up. The woman's voice was like liquid honey. When did she ditch Tamara? she wondered, clearing her throat.

"I have a lesson booked, midafternoon.

Would you tell Jake that I have to cancel? The name is Truman."

Cass hung up, her whole body trembling. Enough was enough—she had to get over Jake and regain her emotional independence. She was in love with him, there was no doubt about that. When—or if—Tara left, maybe there would still be a chance for the two of them, but she wasn't prepared to be second best or wait around like a lovesick idiot.

She'd call in at the clinic, she decided, trying to think of anything other than Jake Munro. She would check up on the stray cat she'd treated yesterday and see if Todd had scheduled time off for her to visit her parents. The cat was little more than a kitten—half-grown, half-starved, dehydrated and close to death. A sorry sight. She'd removed a lump from its neck, checked it over and made it comfortable, but no one really expected it to survive. And if it did recover, what then? Who would want to rehome a scraggy stray?

"Come on, Puddle," she said, gathering her bag and car keys. The pup jumped up, wagging her white-tipped tail. Cass reached down for her, burying her face in her silky coat. "Just you and me, girl," she announced, stepping back out into the murky gray morning. "Even the sunshine has deserted us." She smiled wryly. "But hey, who cares?"

THE MARMALADE-COLORED cat was lying on its side. Its ribcage jutted through its ragged coat and its yellow eyes were dull.

"Hey, little fella," she murmured, opening the cage door. "At least you're alive."

"I reckon it's on the mend now," remarked Todd, who had followed her in. "I'll have to get Animal Concern to come and collect it in a day or two."

"I'll have him."

She'd spoken on impulse, but the more she thought about it, the more certain Cass was. She reached into the cage and gently extracted the pathetic, bony bundle of fur.

"I'll give him a home."

Todd frowned. "If you start taking in all the strays that come in, you'll have a houseful in a month. It's not good policy."

"I didn't think he would survive. He deserves a chance."

"Well, it's your call, but don't say I didn't warn you." He was about to leave the room, but turned back. "Oh, and is next week okay for your time off, say Monday to Thursday? Or did you need a full week?"

"That'll be fine…thanks."

Placing the cat carefully back in its cage, Cass felt a glow of satisfaction. This was what her job was all about—saving lives and mending creatures. She didn't need anything else.

CHAPTER TWENTY

JAKE RETURNED TO Sky View with a heavy heart. His whole being ached for Cass, but he had made a promise to do what was right, for once, and he was determined to see it through. He would have to keep Tara at arm's length. At least he and Cass could still be friends—if that was possible.

That night, sleep was evasive, his head swirling with emotions and strange dreams. He woke as dawn crept over the horizon and went out to do the horses early, avoiding breakfast altogether and concentrating on the youngsters he was schooling. Working with their open, honest dispositions always helped to soothe his soul.

As he was leading the last of the three horses in from the school, Robbie appeared in the yard on his red bike.

"Mum says its lunchtime," he called. "And we've got a surprise for you."

Jake furrowed his brows. "What kind of surprise?"

"You'll have to come and see." Robbie's face gleamed with excitement. "Do you know where Granddad is?"

"No, I haven't seen him. I'll be over in a minute. I just have to put Sam here away."

Having groomed the young chestnut gelding and given him a hay net, Jake headed for the house, his heart buoyant at the thought of spending time with his son. His joy was tempered, however, by the distinct feeling that Tara was up to something. She seemed to have no end of schemes to persuade Jake to let her stay, and he sensed she wasn't being totally honest with him.

"Mum's made a cake," Robbie cried as Jake opened the kitchen door. "And sandwiches!"

A plastic container on the table appeared to be stacked with food, and a large bottle of juice stood beside it.

"We're going on a picnic—a real family picnic. You, me, Mum and Granddad."

"But I have to work, son," Jake said. "And have you even asked your granddad?"

"It's all right." Tara turned to him, a

broad smile on her face. "Your lesson rang and canceled, and we're only going down to the river. Surely you can spare an hour or two…for Robbie."

"Cass, you mean. Cass cancelled?"

"Truman, her name was," Tara said, sounding deliberately vague.

"Please, Dad?" Robbie, butted in, grabbing Jake's hand. "We'll be like a proper family."

Tara shrugged. "It was his idea, not mine. Now go and find your granddad, Rob, and ask him if he wants to come."

Jake watched as Robbie ran into the yard, greeting Bill as he emerged from the barn.

"Pretending isn't the answer," he told Tara. "He'll only get his hopes up and then be disappointed…again. That's worse than being disappointed in the first place."

She stared at him like she used to, with eyes full of passion and promise. "Maybe this time he won't be disappointed," she murmured, just as Robbie came racing back inside.

"Granddad says he'll come," he yelled, his eyes shining. "And you, Dad? Will you come, too?"

Jake hesitated. "Yes," he agreed finally, with an awkward glance at Tara. He saw triumph in her eyes. "I'll come...for you, Rob."

CASS CALLED HER parents as soon as she got home from the surgery. She didn't expect her news about visiting to generate a flood of tears.

"It's supposed to be a good thing," she told her mum, smiling. She felt guilty for leaving the trip for so long.

"It *is* a good thing," her mum said, laughing through the tears. "When? What time will you be here, and how long can you stay?"

After she put down the phone, it occurred to Cass how lucky she was to be able to rely on her parents' love and support. As a kid, she had resented how busy they were, but they were always there for her, totally non-judgmental and proud of her no matter what she did. Not everyone had that kind of backup—certainly not Robbie. His whole life was a confused mess.

Suddenly sure of her decision to stay

away from Jake and the stables, she wondered if perhaps it was time to give up the
cottage, too. Staying around here was prov-
ing to be too painful. Maybe it was time to
move on. She could even apply for a new
job—somewhere that specialized in horses.

When Robbie's beaming face appeared
in her doorway as the shadows were beginning to lengthen, Cass was even more convinced that she was doing the right thing
by staying away from Sky View.

"Guess what," he said, bursting into the
kitchen and making a beeline for Puddle.

"What?" she asked.

"We've all been on a family picnic."

Bess stood in the open doorway, whining
softly. A falcon screeched in the blue sky
beyond, and a solitary sheep bleated loudly
in the meadow, missing its lambs. Simple,
normal everyday sounds that somehow
screamed inside Cass's head.

She cleared her throat loudly, trying to
find the right response. "A *family* picnic,
eh?"

He nodded happily. "Me, Mum, Dad
and Granddad. We went down to the river
with cake and sandwiches and everything.

Granddad brought a ball and we all played football. It was great."

"So you think your mum will be staying around for a while, then?"

Setting Puddle carefully back on the ground, Robbie turned to her with a secretive smile that gradually spread across his whole face, showing her a new side of this reserved and sad little boy.

"Oh, yes," he cried. "I think they might get married again, and then I'll *never* have to leave Sky View."

For a moment, Cass struggled to breathe. "No matter what happens, Rob," she told him when she found her voice. "Your dad will never let anyone take you away from here again."

He tilted his head to one side. "You think so?"

She took hold of both his hands, trying to push away her heartache and absorb his joy. "I know so," she said.

CASS LEFT THE marmalade cat recovering at the surgery while she took time off to visit her parents. Todd gave her another lecture about getting attached to her patients when she stopped by the clinic to say goodbye on her way past.

"It's a professional lesson you have to learn," he told her, as she gently stroked the mangy creature. "Do your best for them, but don't become personally involved."

She smiled, taking in what he was telling her and instantly dismissing it. "I get where you're coming from, Todd, but that's just not me. It was my passion to help animals that got me into this business in the first place. I can't help but get involved."

Todd shook his gray head slowly. "Then you're in for a world of heartbreak, I'm afraid—and possibly a house full of strays. For what it's worth, though, I admire your passion. Have a good break, and I'll see you on the weekend. Oh, and how was your visit to the stud the other day?"

Cass smiled. "It was wonderful," she said.

"And you still want to specialize in horses?"

"Even more so."

"Then speak to me when you get back. I saw a course advertised in the monthly veterinary manual, to bring vets up to date with the latest equestrian treatments. I'm sure Donald will want to attend, and I thought you might like to go with him."

Cass clasped her hands together like an excited teenager. "I'd love to."

"I figured," Todd replied, laughing.

THE EXPRESSION ON her parents' faces when Cass had arrived home had made the journey so worthwhile, Cass reflected as she walked Puddle along the riverbank where she used to go with Bud. She'd been home since the day before yesterday, and already it felt like she'd never left.

"So," her father had said when she and Puddle had jumped out of the car. "You've finally got another dog."

"It's taken a while," she responded.

"I'll say. I never thought you'd get over Bud."

"I never really have," she admitted. "But it's thanks to him that I've got my career."

A couple of days reliving her childhood was exactly what she'd needed, Cass thought. Everything seemed to have slipped into perspective, helping her to rediscover the original passion that had driven her to become a vet, even if it had caused a few tears along the way.

Her parents had welcomed her with such joy, and her mother had even taken a few hours off to go out for lunch with her yesterday. She remembered their conversation as she sat on a log, watching the timeless flow of the river just as she had done so often as a child. Her mother had asked about her life, and for once, Cass felt comfortable opening up a little, even telling her mum briefly about Jake and Robbie.

"Do what your heart tells you is right," her mother had advised. "Go with your instinct."

Standing up, Cass grabbed a stick and hurled it for Puddle. Her instinct was to get as far away from Sky View as possible. As soon as she got back to Little Dale, she was going to see Bill about moving out. And maybe she *should* think about leaving the practice. Sticking around to watch Jake play happy family would drive her crazy.

She would be setting off the next morning. Though she was reluctant to say goodbye to her parents, she felt much more positive. She had the equestrian course to look forward to, and she would pick up the marmalade cat on her way back to the cottage. The poor thing needed some love and attention as soon as possible.

PUDDLE DIDN'T KNOW what to make of Marmalade. The half-grown cat hissed loudly from his box on the front seat while the pup whined and yapped in the back.

"I'll take you back to the surgery," she warned him, laughing and stroking his rough fur. Marmalade went quiet instantly, desperate for attention, and her heart turned over. "Don't worry, you're part of our family now, and you're not going anywhere, no matter what happens."

The cottage seemed welcoming, warm and familiar—a real home, Cass thought. Steeling her heart, she dialed Bill's number before she could change her mind.

"So tell me what you've really rung me for?" he asked after their initial small talk. "No heating, perhaps? Or, don't tell me… you've got a leak."

"No, it's nothing like that," Cass said. "I…I could just do with a chat, that's all."

"Oh, dear, that sounds ominous. Do you want me to stop by?"

"Yes, if you don't mind. I'd rather speak to you in person."

"Right, then."

Was it disappointment she detected in his tone?

BILL ARRIVED WHILE Cass was outside with Puddle.

"Sorry," she called, hurrying toward him. He was sitting on the bench outside the front door, waiting for her. "I only went a little way up the lane. Thanks for coming so promptly."

Bill made a fuss over the cat while Cass put on the kettle and brewed a pot of tea.

"I must say it is an odd-looking creature," he remarked, smiling. "But no doubt you'll soon have it fat and glossy again."

She deposited two mugs on the table and sat down beside him.

"Todd wasn't too pleased about me taking it in, but I just couldn't resist. It's hardly more than a kitten, and it must have fended for itself for weeks. All it needs is a bit of love and attention."

"That applies to all of us, I guess," Bill said sadly. "Poor Robbie could do with some, that's for sure."

"But he's got lots of love," Cass said. "There's you and Jake and…his mum."

"He does now, it's just… To be honest, Cass, we're really worried about him."

"I've met him a couple of times," she confessed. "He seems like such a bright little boy. A bit sad, I suppose."

"Oh, he is bright, but I think he's been bottling up his feelings for a long time. He hasn't accepted that his gran and Lucy are dead, you know, and he wakes up with terrible nightmares."

Cass could tell Bill was struggling to hold back a rush of emotion. "He keeps running away…"

"And is Tara back for good?" Cass couldn't help asking.

Bill shrugged. "Who knows what Tara's intentions are? Anyway…" He looked directly at Cass, changing the subject. "What did you really want to see me about?"

Cass gazed down to where her hands rested in her lap. "I'm afraid I'm going to have to hand in my notice on the cottage."

"What! You're saying you want to leave? But why? I thought you loved it here."

"Things have changed," she explained, blinking back tears. "I need to be in the village, closer to the surgery…"

She met Bill's eyes, surprised to see sadness in them. They were so like Jake's that she felt something twist deep inside her. "To be honest," she said, voicing the vague idea that had been flitting around in her head. "I'm even thinking about applying for another job, somewhere where I can get more specialized equine experience…"

Bill held her gaze, and she had the distinct impression that he could see straight through her excuses.

"I do love it here, you know," she mumbled. "And you've been great. It's just…"

"Look…" He placed his hand gently on her arm. "I really don't want you to go, but you have to do what's right for you. You have a six-month contract, but I won't hold you to that. Just stay until the end of the month—to take the time to reconsider."

"Thank you," she managed. "This way, you'll have time to look for another tenant, too."

"Exactly," he agreed. "And Cass?"

"Yes?"

"Don't give up on Jake."

"I think he's the one who's given up on me," she said. "Not that there was anything to give up on in the first place." She stood up, forcing a smile onto her face. "I don't really care either way. I have a lot going on at work, that's all. It will be more convenient to be closer, and I have my career to think about. I do love it here at Sky View," she said again. "But I think it's just time to move on."

"Well, make sure it's for the right reasons," Bill advised. "There are still two and a half weeks until the end of the month, so you'll have time to change your mind if you like. Promise me you'll think long and hard about it."

"I promise," she said, relieved that their conversation was over. Somehow, Bill Munro had a way of making her question her own decisions.

CASS HAD AN early start the next morning, after a call came in from a truck driver who'd found some abandoned, half-dead pups on the hard shoulder of the M6. She checked on Marmalade, pleased to see that he'd eaten all his food from the night before and used his litter tray.

"I'll be back this afternoon," she said, petting the scrawny cat.

Marmalade stared at her with huge amber eyes before curling up in his basket, happy to have a warm bed and food in his belly at last.

The trucker was waiting at the highway exit. She saw him as soon as she pulled up.

"Sorry to bother you," he said. "I'm just passing through on my way south, but when I saw them I had to stop, and a local vet seemed the most obvious person to call. I don't know what you do about payment in a case like this. I mean…well, they're not mine, but I couldn't just leave them to die, and I don't think they'd have lasted until I got home.

"That's fine. Don't worry about it."

Cass glanced inside the cardboard box. Three pairs of bright, anxious eyes looked back at her. The fourth pair was dull and drained of life.

"Thanks for caring," she told the driver. "I don't know how people can be so cruel."

With a lift of his hand, the man took his leave.

By the time Cass got the puppies back to the surgery, one of them had already died. Anger and grief overwhelmed her. How many days of life had the poor little creature had? Virtually none. How could someone go about his daily life with such a crime on his conscience?

She was treating the other three pups when Donald arrived at eight o'clock.

"Turning into an animal rescue sanctuary now, are we?" He smiled. "Todd won't be happy."

"I'll pay for them myself if I have to," she said. "I became a vet to save lives, not to make money."

"Good on you, girl," he told her. "Getting too involved can be a mistake, though."

"Let me guess," she sighed. "He's told you about Marmalade."

"Marmalade?"

"The cat."

"Ah, yes. The cat."

"Did he ask you to have a word with me?"

"Something like that. But Cass…"

Settling the three puppies in a free kennel, she looked up at him.

"Never stop caring."

"No one could stop me," she said.

THE REST OF the morning passed uneventfully. Todd groaned when he saw the pups.

"We're not a charity, Cass. It's a job for Animal Concern, really. You'd better give them a ring—not that I don't appreciate you going to the rescue, mind."

She shrugged. "I was on call, and they needed help."

As she gave the puppies one last check and gently placed them back in the crate to await collection, an idea came to her. She picked up the smallest, a cheeky-looking white dog with three brown spots on its back and one over its eye, and moved it into another cage.

Cass was in the operating room when the rescue center worker arrived.

Jill, the new receptionist, put her head around the door. "Is it just the two pups in the box to go?" she asked.

Cass nodded, loading her syringe. "Yes,

the brown-and-white one is going some-where else."

Cass left the surgery at two, hoping Todd wouldn't notice the box she was carrying. If he thought she was rescuing another stray, he'd be questioning her profession-alism altogether. The pup whined softly as she placed it in her car. In her bed on the back seat, Puddle pricked up her ears.

"Don't worry, girl," Cass said, laughing. "He isn't taking your place.

Back at the cottage, Marmalade was ob-viously feeling better. He purred when he saw Cass come through the door, eagerly lapping up the milk she poured him.

"It's like a home for orphans and strays around here," Cass said, feeling a sudden wrench. The cottage had become a real home—to her and the animals—and the thought of having to leave it made her ache.

The abandoned puppy cowered in the corner of his box, missing the comfort of his siblings, distrustful of the whole world.

Cass tried to read a book on Thorough-bred studs for the next hour or so, but she kept glancing out the window and losing her place on the page. Eventually she gave up, but as she reached for Puddle's lead she finally saw Robbie approach. She waited eagerly as he pushed his bike down the path and leaned it carefully against the wall.

"Hello," she said brightly when his head appeared around the kitchen door.

He smiled at her—*just like any ordinary six-year-old,* she thought.

"Granddad says you've got a cat."

"News travels fast."

"Can I see it?"

She stood back, motioning him in. He peered down at Marmalade.

"Can I pick it up?"

"Definitely. He'd love a cuddle."

He sat on a chair, nursing the mangy cat, thoughtfully tracing his ribs with his finger.

"Why did you want such an ugly, scruffy cat?" he asked, looking up at Cass.

"Life isn't all about being beautiful, Robbie," she told him. "We're all God's creatures, no matter what we look like, and we all deserve to be happy and cared for and loved. I saved his life, and now I want to make it a good one."

"Am I one of God's creatures, too?" he asked.

"Of course you are," she said, dropping down on her knees beside him. "It isn't just animals. All of us are God's creatures—me, you, your dad and granddad…and your mum."

Robbie stared at her with such grief in his eyes that her heart turned over.

"And Lucy and Gran? Are they God's creatures, too?"

"Yes, Robbie, they are."

"Then why didn't someone save *their* lives and look after them? Why didn't God love them?"

"Oh, Robbie…"

All of a sudden the little boy was in her arms, sobbing against her shoulder, huge wracking gasps that tore her apart.

"God did love Lucy and your gran," she said. "He loved them so much that He took them to Heaven early, because He wanted them to be with Him."

Robbie's sobs subsided.

"And He's taking care of them there, in Heaven?"

"Oh, yes. He's taking care of them very

well. They're both watching over you, too, so you need to make them proud of you. Here…" Taking him by the hand, she led him to the corner of the room. "I have something for you."

Robbie's eyes shone. "It's a puppy," he cried.

"It's *your* puppy," she said. "But we'll have to ask your dad first."

"Did you save its life, too?"

"Yes," she said, as he reached down to pick up the tiny creature. "I saved his life, but I want you to take care of him and make it a good one."

"It'll be the best ever," he promised. "Can I go and ask Dad now?"

Cass had thought as far as this moment but not beyond it. "Let's wait until he's a bit stronger before you take him home," she suggested. "But you can come and see him whenever you want."

Robbie cradled the pup in his arms, his heart all over his face as he beamed up at Cass.

"I'm going to call him Chocolate… Choco for short, because his spots look like

chocolate drops. Your eyes are like chocolate drops, too."

Cass smiled, choking back tears. "That's
a lovely thing to say."

CHAPTER TWENTY-ONE

JAKE JUMPED DOWN from the big black youngster he was schooling, absentmindedly running his hand along its neck. Since the picnic, his head had been in turmoil. Tara might have claimed that staying at Sky View and pretending to be a family was for Robbie's sake, but he had the distinct impression that she wanted something more permanent than that. Then again, he thought, why would she? She was talented and famous, so why would she want to retrieve a relationship that was long gone? Maybe he was just imagining the way she looked at him or being cynical—perhaps she really did regret leaving them, and now, just like him, she truly wanted to do what was right for their son.

Last night, after Robbie had gone to bed and before his dad came home from a meeting in town, she had brought a drink to his office, handing it to him with an open smile and perching on the edge of his desk.

"Have you thought about what I suggested, Jake?" she asked.

He had responded with a shrug, taking a gulp of his drink before answering her question. "If you mean your idea about pretending to be a family, then no. It's a crazy idea," he told her firmly.

She had held his gaze with a disconcerting passion in her eyes. "Look," she pleaded. "I know it's not what you'd planned, but this isn't about us—this is for Robbie. We owe him, Jake, we owe him big time. Did you see him at the picnic? He was a normal, happy little boy again, and I for one would do anything to keep him like that."

His reply had been fuelled by anger. "What, and you think I wouldn't?"

She had responded to his outburst by sliding off the desk and leaning toward him. "I don't know," she said. "You tell me."

"I would do anything for Robbie," he had insisted, meaning it.

Her familiar scent had filled his nostrils as her lips hovered near his.

"Well, there you are then," she had murmured, kissing him softly on the cheek. "This is your chance to prove it—to make up to him for…everything. Remember what we once had, Jake? It wasn't all bad, was it?"

"No, Tara," he replied instantly. "It wasn't all bad, but those times are gone, in the past."

"Then we can make new times, for Robbie. I know it may not work out, but at least we would have tried to do the right thing."

Jake mulled over their conversation as he untacked the horse and turned him loose with an affectionate pat. For just a moment, a brief, crazy moment, he imagined the expression on Robbie's face if he thought his dad and mum were going to try and make a go of it again. That was what the boy really needed—some stability in his life. It had been turned upside down when his gran and Lucy were taken away from him in one cruel swoop, and he hadn't even had the chance to properly grieve because his mother had whisked him away from all that was familiar. Either Tara had to get out of their lives as soon as possible, or.... No, he couldn't believe he was actually considering the idea, not even for Rob.

As Jake walked out of the stable into the autumn sunshine, his head in a whirl, he saw Robbie ride his bike through the gate. The boy certainly had enjoyed the picnic, he reflected. It had been good to see his son relax and enjoy himself for once. Although, come to think of it, he seemed pretty happy right now.

"You look like you've had a good time," Jake called.

Dropping his bike, Robbie sprinted toward him, a bright smile on his face.

"Guess what," he cried.

Jake headed into the tack room with Robbie running along behind.

"Go on then, surprise me."

"I might be getting a puppy...if you'll let me. We'll be a proper family then. All proper families have dogs."

There's that proper family idea again. Jake's half-formed idea popped into his head again as he gazed down at the boy's radiant expression.

"You've got Bess," he said. "She's your dog, remember?"

Robbie's face fell. "I love Bess, I really do, but she's your dog, really. I'd like a pup all of my own"

Jake ruffled his son's hair, hard put to deny him anything. "Well, then, I guess we'll have to get you one."

"I already have one. Well, kind of."

Jake raised his eyebrows. "Has Granddad put you up to this?"

"No, I haven't seen Granddad."

"Then who?"

"The lady with chocolate eyes has a puppy. She rescued him, and he needs someone to look after him."

Jake felt a band squeezing around his chest. "You've seen Cass, from the cottage?"

Robbie nodded. "She's nice to me, and she says I can have the pup when he's a bit stronger, if you'll let me."

"Well, if she's serious, I suppose we can think about it. We can start your riding lessons again, too."

"Thanks, Dad, that would be great. I'll go and tell her."

"Not right now." Jake smiled. "You can go tomorrow. How did it come up, anyway, about the pup? Where did you see her?" Suddenly, it felt so important to Jake to find out how Robbie had met Cass. He liked the idea of them spending time together, but it brought an ache of longing for what might have been with him and Cass…what still could be.

Robbie shrugged. "When I was out on my bike."

"Are you sure about that?"

"She's my friend," Robbie said.

Jake ruffled his hair. "I'm glad to hear that, Rob. She's a very nice lady."

Robbie grinned. "I know she is."

TRUE TO HER current form, Tara already had dinner on the table when Jake and Robbie finished in the yard. The boy had helped empty wheelbarrows, filled all the hay nets and swept the whole yard by himself.

"What do you think, Dad?" Jake had said when Bill arrived to find his grandson heaving a loaded barrow onto the muck heap. "We'll have to put him on the payroll."

"I don't know how we managed without him." Bill chuckled.

The three of them had entered the kitchen feeling a sense of camaraderie— a true sense of how it used to be before their world turned upside down. It had been his mum making dinner then, though, not Tara. And if Jake was honest with himself, he hadn't even been around that much. He owed it to Robbie to get things right this time, and he couldn't afford to mess up.

Tara met his gaze, her flawless face glowing. For once, she had ditched the stylish clothes and was wearing a simple floral dress.

"Sit down," she insisted. "I've done a nice roast."

Suddenly, to Jake, the whole scene seemed superficial. There was more to Tara's behavior than she was letting on. He was sure of it.

THAT EVENING, AFTER Robbie went up to bed, Bill, Jake and Tara sat awkwardly together, watching TV.

"I'm going to check on the bay three-year-old," Jake muttered, stifled by the atmosphere. "It had a bit of colic earlier."

"I have some work to do, too," Bill chimed in, following him through the kitchen. "The builders are starting on Monday. In fact..." He placed a hand on Jake's arm. "I've been meaning to ask you for a while. I'm not as young as I was, and I'd really like you on board with this project."

Jake frowned, pausing as he reached for his jacket.

"What, me? A builder?"

"Not exactly. I was thinking more project management. I can do all the mundane stuff, but it would be nice to have someone to run ideas past."

Jake considered the idea. "I'd be proud to, Dad," he said.

"We'll go through the plans tomorrow, then," Bill suggested. "And I hope the youngster's okay. Give me a call if you need a hand. Oh, and...." He hesitated.

"Yes?" prompted Jake.

"Be careful, won't you? Don't make any quick decisions you might regret."

As he crossed the yard, Jake sensed a movement behind him. Suddenly, he felt a hand on his arm, holding him back. He jumped, spinning around.

"Tara? What are you doing out here?"

"I need to talk to you, Jake."

There was an urgency in her tone that unnerved him.

"Go on then, what do you want to say?"

"I was serious, you know…about giving us another go."

His response was instant. "I've thought about it, Tara, and it's too late. It didn't work last time and it wouldn't work now. You'd be hankering after fame and success again, and where would that leave Robbie?"

"Please, Jake. At least consider the idea. I've changed, I really have. Fame and success aren't quite what I imagined they would be, and I'm ready to settle down now."

She wrapped her arms around him, lifting her face toward his, her expression needy. He hesitated, overcome by the moment, all the memories flooding back—the first time they met, their wedding day….

"No!" He pulled away. "Stop this, Tara. It isn't fair."

"Please tell me you'll think about it," she begged.

"I'll think about it," he said reluctantly. "But now I have a sick horse to see to."

THE ELEGANT BAY was down, thrashing about in its straw bed, lathered with sweat.

Jake reached for his phone.

BILL SAW TARA follow Jake outside, and his stomach sank. She wanted to get back together with him—there was no doubt in his mind about that. Right now, Jake would do anything for Robbie. Bill heaved a heavy sigh and went back to studying the plans that were spread out in front of him on the office table. His son was old enough to make his own decisions, even though they might be flawed by guilt and regret.

Tara was a very different kettle of fish. Why would anyone so wealthy and famous give up her career to bury herself in the heart of the Lake District? She had a hidden agenda, he was sure of it, something she wasn't telling them, but there was no way he was going to sit back and watch his family fall apart all over again. She might be playing the sympathy card with Jake, but Bill wasn't convinced.

He had promised to go up and see Robbie before he fell asleep. He'd have a chat with the boy, he decided, ask him a few subtle questions about living in America.

Bill knocked gently on Robbie's bedroom door before pushing it open to find him eagerly waiting.

"It's okay, Granddad," he said. "I'm not asleep. I thought you'd forgotten."

The old man sat down on the side of the bed. "As if I'd forget about you."

The little boy looked thoughtful. "Did you forget about me when I was living with mum?"

"No, Rob, we missed you all the time. We could never forget you. Did you like it in America?"

Robbie shrugged. "It was okay. We went to Disney World and stuff."

"With your mum's friend?"

"Yes, he was nice."

"Your mum said you weren't very happy there."

The little boy gazed up at him, a wistful expression on his face.

"I missed Dad and you such a lot…and Lucy and Gran. I can say that now because I know, so it's okay to talk about them."

"What do you know, Rob?"

A happy smile brought new warmth to the boy's pinched features. "I just wanted them back. Mum told me they died and I knew it couldn't be true. I was so cross all the time, and then she told me we were coming home. I was happy because I thought they'd be here."

A sharp pain twisted inside Bill's chest. "And now?" he asked.

"Now I know that God is looking after them both in Heaven, and Lucy has Gran to look after her, too. They had to go because they were special. He loved them so much that He couldn't wait for them anymore. They're watching over us, though, so we have to try and make them proud."

Bill turned his face away, trying to control a rush of emotion. He looked back, blinking away tears.

"How do you know all this, Robbie?"

The little boy hesitated, not wanting to answer.

"Someone must have talked to you. Was it your dad?"

He shook his head, his mouth pressed into a firm line. "It's a secret."

"Well, I'm not going to make you give up your secret, Rob, but will you tell whoever it was that they've got a big thank-you from me for helping you?"

"Yes, I will," Robbie responded happily. "Can we go see their special place at the church? Mum told me there's a stone for them there."

"There's a beautiful stone, Rob. We'll go there tomorrow."

"With Dad?"

"If you like. Are you sure you don't want to tell me who you've been talking to, though?"

The little boy snuggled down under his duvet. "Maybe, but I'll have to ask her first."

Her. So it had to be Tara, didn't it? But she was no secret.

"Night, Rob," he murmured, planting a kiss on the boy's forehead and realizing that he was already asleep.

CHAPTER TWENTY-TWO

CASS HEARD THE phone from upstairs and raced down to answer it. She'd just come in from a false alarm and didn't feel like going out again already. Reluctantly, she picked up the receiver.

"Hello?" she began.

"I have an emergency."

Jake's deep, urgent tone, instantly recognizable, made her tremble. Angry with herself for her reaction she answered abruptly, her voice clear and clipped, totally impartial.

"Yes, it's Cass Truman. I'm the vet on call tonight."

The line went quiet and she heard Jake clear his throat.

"What's the problem?" she asked.

"It's me, Cass. Jake. I have a horse with colic. Can you come right away?"

She hung up the phone with a strong

sense of déjà vu, desperately hoping that this time the situation would have a better outcome.

BILL APPEARED IN the stable doorway, wanting to talk to Jake but realizing right away that the time was far from right.

"Have you called the vet?" he asked, digging in his pocket for his cell.

Jake nodded. "It's okay, Dad. She's on her way."

"She?"

"Yes. Cass is on call."

Their eyes, so similar, caught and glanced away. Bill knew they were both thinking of Rosie but reluctant to put their thoughts into words.

Cass arrived five minutes later, taking over with a calm confidence. Moving quickly and carefully, she ran her hands across the nervous youngster's body, putting him at ease.

"There, boy, we'll soon have you right as rain again," she murmured. "How long has he been like this?" she asked Jake, her tone purely professional.

"Not long," he replied. "It's worsened in the last half hour."

She nodded. "His temperature isn't too high, so I'll give him a muscle relaxant and something for the pain. Has he passed anything?"

The two men glanced at each other in relief.

"Yes," said Jake. "I think so."

"Then I'm pretty sure it's just flatulent colic, nothing serious. He's uncomfortable, but I don't think there's anything to worry about. Keep an eye on him, and give me a ring if it doesn't ease up soon. I'll call back in the morning anyway, just to be sure."

"What? Are you on all night and tomorrow?"

Cass's face remained passive. "Of course not." She smiled. "But I like to follow things through."

"Can I get you a coffee?" Bill asked, wanting to leave the two of them alone without being too obvious.

Cass didn't seem to pick up on the opportunity.

"No, thanks," she replied. "I'd better get moving."

Jake and Bill watched her turn and walk away.

"Thanks," Jake called after her.

A heavy silence fell after she'd gone, broken only by the sound of her car as it disappeared down the lane. When it faded into the distance, Bill looked determinedly across to where his son was busying himself with the sick horse.

"You do know she's leaving, don't you?"

Jake froze. "Leaving? But why… What do you mean?"

"You tell me."

"Leaving the practice?"

"Possibly, but she definitely wants to give up the cottage at the end of the month."

"But you can't let her—she has a six-month contract."

Bill took his son's arm, looking him full in the face.

"You could stop her," he said. "If you really wanted to."

Jake's face was ashen. "You know I can't do that right now."

"You owe Tara nothing, Jake."

"But I do owe Robbie."

"And if things go wrong again, then where does that leave him? It's about you, too, Jake, and Robbie isn't stupid. Anyway,

I think he may finally have begun to move on. He told me some things tonight…"

"What kind of things?"

"You need to talk to him yourself, but I really think he's coming to terms with losing Lucy and your mum. He's going to be okay, Jake, I'm sure of it."

"Tara seems to feel we should carry on playing happy family for Robbie's sake," Jake told him.

"For her own sake, you mean," Bill said. "I'm not saying she doesn't love Robbie—of course she does, but I'm not convinced her motives are sincere. Talk to her, Jake, get the truth out of her before you make any rash decisions. If you did give it another go, and then split up again, it would be ten times worse for Robbie."

JAKE STAYED WITH the bay gelding for another half hour. *Get the truth out of Tara,* his dad had said. Was there really something she wasn't telling him? Could she really have a motive other than her total change of heart and her wish to finally do what was best for their son? And what about her career? How did her singing figure into all this?

"You'll be okay, now, boy," he told the big horse as it stood resting, a hind leg locked and eyes half-shut.

Carefully bolting the stable door behind him, Jake stepped into the moonlit night, staring along the lane toward Sky Cottage. Would Cass be in bed by now? he wondered. Maybe she'd had another call. He should have spoken to her. Then again, what could he have said? Even he didn't know what was going on with his life at the moment. In the morning, he'd have a chat with Robbie and find out for himself what his dad had meant about the boy coming to terms with things.

Jake woke at five-thirty, his mind still going around in circles. Work, he decided, climbing out of bed, was the best remedy for anything. And he needed to check on the bay.

The big horse whinnied when he saw Jake approach, tossing his handsome head over the stable door. Jake checked him over, relieved to find that he'd totally recovered, then he tied up a hay net for him before starting on the beds.

He was on his fourth stall when he heard a car in the lane. It must be Cass. Resisting the temptation to put down his fork and go rushing out to greet her, he continued leveling the straw bed.

"Hi."

Her voice over the stable door made his heart leap. He looked up, feigning surprise.

"Oh, hi. I didn't hear you coming. You'll be pleased to know that Micky seems to have made a total recovery."

She smiled—an open, honest smile that brought a warm glow to her ivory skin.

"Good. I thought he would have. You'd have called if he hadn't. I guess I didn't really need to stop by, but…"

"I'm glad you did," Jake interrupted her, slipping out the door and sliding the bolt behind him. He towered over her slight frame, wanting to reach out his hand, to touch her one more time.

She turned away abruptly.

"I'll have a quick look at him anyway."

"Cass…"

She stopped in her tracks as he said her name.

"We need to talk," Jake began.

She held his gaze, revealing nothing.

"No, Jake," she retorted. "We don't need to talk. Whatever we thought we had can never happen. You have Robbie…and Tara to think about now, and I'm happy for you. I really am."

Suddenly, she reached up to plant a gentle kiss on his cheek. He took her hand in his but she pulled it away.

"Bye, Jake."

As he watched her walk away his heart slowly tore in two.

ROBBIE WANDERED OUT of the house at eight, rubbing his bleary eyes.

"What time do you call this, son?" Jake smiled. "I'm almost done."

"Sorry, Dad."

"That's okay—you need your beauty sleep."

They worked in silence for a while, filling the last of the hay nets. Jake wondered how and when to approach what his dad had mentioned last night. Perhaps he should leave it until after breakfast.

"Will you come with us to the church this morning, Dad? Please say you will."

Robbie's plea took him completely by surprise. "The church…" he stammered. "But why?"

"I want to see the beautiful stone. Lucy and Gran's stone."

A painful lump lodged itself in Jake's throat.

"So you'll come?"

He looked at Robbie, so like his twin sister—so like himself.

"Of course I'll come, Rob. But why now, after all this time?"

"Because now I know."

"Know what, Rob?"

"I know that Lucy and Gran have gone to Heaven because God wanted them to be with Him there. And I know they're watching over us every day. We'll be able to talk to them at their special place."

Robbie smiled, taking hold of his father's hand. Jake squeezed it tightly, never wanting to let go.

"How do you know all this, Rob?"

"I saw her ugly cat. She told me it didn't matter that it was ugly because it's one of God's creatures and He loves them all no matter what they look like. We're all God's creatures, and He loves us all no matter what, even if we're bad. He loved Gran and Lucy so much, he sent for them early. That's why they had to go."

"How often do you see Cass?" asked Jake, dropping down to Robbie's eye level.

"How did you know?" Robbie cried. "She's my friend…my *secret* friend."

"I just guessed, but I won't tell anyone," promised Jake. "Now come on, let's go find your mum and granddad."

JAKE FELT A warm rush of love and pride as he, Robbie, Bill and Tara stood by the headstone. Robbie held both their hands, talking to his sister and his gran in a matter-of-fact way, as if they were right there listening to him. He told them all about America and how happy he was to be back home at Sky View, and how much he missed them both. For the first time in more than twelve long months, Jake finally felt some closure and a lessening of the pain and guilt that had colored his whole being.

Knowing now, with a new certainty, exactly where he wanted his life to go, he decided to talk to Tara that night, as soon as Robbie was in bed. His opportunity, however, came sooner than expected.

After their visit to the churchyard, Jake worked three horses and turned them out into the far meadow before coming back to the office for a meeting with his dad's architect. He was surprised by how interesting he found the building project, and decided he was looking forward to his new role as Bill's right-hand man. When Shane Price, the forward-thinking young architect they had hired, finally left with his laptop under his arm, Bill turned to Jake.

"Some pretty good ideas, eh?"

Jake nodded. "Yes, I think it's going to look great if we can get it past the planners."

"Well, Shane is supposed to be whiz at that. Anyway, I'm off."

"Where are you going?"

"I told you, I promised to take Robbie swimming. You can come if you like."

Seeing his moment, Jake shook his head.

"Another time, perhaps. I have something important to do."

Bill raised his eyebrows. "Anything I should know about?"

"Not yet. I'll see you when you get back. Have fun."

Not wanting to waste any more time now that he'd made up his mind, Jake ducked back inside as soon as Bill's four-by-four disappeared down the drive with an ecstatic Robbie waving from the window.

He found Tara in the kitchen, stirring something in a pan. The whole place smelled temptingly of beef stew, and for a second he felt himself waver. She was going to so much trouble to try and make this work...for Robbie. Remembering how it had been before...what she had done, he hardened his heart.

"Tara, we need to talk."

As if on cue, her voice floated out from the radio, her heartrending tones flooding his ears. Stepping quickly forward, he flicked off the switch and the sound died.

She looked at him in disappointment.

"I thought you'd got past that."

"We need to talk. Please, sit down."

Silence filled the room, empty and total. Jake cleared his throat.

"It's no good, Tara. We can't go backward. Whatever we had when we met is gone, and all this new emotion of yours is just insecurity."

Her cheeks paled beneath her tan. "But what about Robbie? I thought we were going to try and make it work again, for him?"

Jake took both her hands in his. "And how long can you keep up this act? You never baked or made meals like this when we were together. This isn't you, Tara, and within weeks you'd be longing for your glamorous life again."

Fat tears oozed from her beautiful eyes, running down her cheeks and leaving trails of makeup.

"But I can't go back, Jake."

"What do you mean, you can't go back? You're Tamara, the famous and talented singer. And you don't need to go back— you can go anywhere you want."

Her head dropped into her hands, her long, blond hair falling across her face.

"I came back to England because JJ and I broke up, and then I had a huge fight with my manager. I came back here to get some space for a while, but then I got to thinking about how things used to be with us and…"

"Ah," Jake murmured with a new glimmer of understanding. "Now we're getting to the truth of it. Your cozy world turned on its head, so you thought you'd run away and hide where no one could find you. Look, Tara…"

Raising her chin with his thumb and forefinger, he brushed the hair from her face. "Running away isn't the answer—I've found that out the hard way. Besides, hiding here would bore you to death in weeks. Call this manager of yours and sort things out with him. And when you have your career back on track, maybe you and this JJ guy can get back together, too. You obviously still like him…and I know Robbie thinks he's okay."

"He does?"

"That's what he told me."

"And what about Robbie, where does he come in all this?"

"Robbie will be fine with me, here at

Sky View. You can visit, or he can come and stay with you if he wants to, during school holidays. Now pull yourself together, and go sort out your life."

"What will we tell Robbie?"

"The truth, of course. We'll do it together, as soon as he comes back. Now I have a horse to work. You should go and call your manager."

Tara smiled, wiping away her tears. "You always could hide in your riding. I never had that to fall back on."

"You've got your singing," he told her. "You just need to get the rest of your life in order."

CHAPTER TWENTY-THREE

JAKE WALKED SLOWLY along the lane, breathing in the cool evening air as if he'd never really noticed it before, greeting every single sound and scent with newfound sensitivity.

When Robbie had come home from swimming, full of excitement, he and Tara had sat down to talk to him, trying to treat him like an adult and tell him the truth.

Jake had begun by getting straight to the point. "How would you feel, Rob, if your mother went off to take up her singing career again and left you here, with me and Granddad?"

Robbie had just stared at him for a while, his blue eyes huge, and then he'd looked across at Tara. "And will you go see JJ, too?"

"Perhaps," she'd replied. "It depends on how things go."

"And you're not getting back with Dad?"

"I'm afraid not, Robbie. Does that make you sad?"

"A bit, but it's okay. I don't like it when you fight. I do want to stay here, though. You'll come back and see me, won't you?"

Tara had wrapped her arms around him then in the most spontaneous display of emotion Jake had ever seen from her.

"Oh, yes, Rob," she cried. "Of course I'll come and see you. And you can visit me."

The little boy stiffened in her arms. "Just for a holiday, though?"

"Just for a holiday," she promised.

Jake's heart had flipped right over when Robbie caught his eye, as if sharing a secret.

"I'll probably have my own pony by then," he told her proudly. "And a puppy. I'll have both of them to take care of, so I can't be away for too long."

"You'll definitely have your own pony by then, Rob," Jake had said. "In fact, we're going to see one tomorrow, so you'll need an early night."

Once decided, Tara had been set on going as soon as possible. She'd started packing as soon as she got off the phone with her manager. Although he was convinced she was doing the right thing, Jake had been surprised by the speed of her actions.

"I canceled some gigs, you see, when I decided to bring Robbie here. I didn't know how long we…I'd be staying," she'd admitted. "That's why Louis was so angry. Anyway, he wants me back as soon as possible and he says we'll be able to keep the one next month if I start practicing right away."

Jake had taken both her hands in his. "For what it's worth, I think you're making the right call. Getting back together for Robbie's sake would have been the worst decision we ever made. You have to move forward in life, not back."

They had all stood waving when Tara drove away in her bright yellow sports car, and she waved back as if she didn't have a care in the world, all glitz and glamour again, her mind fixed firmly back on her career.

Jake had glanced down at Robbie, and when the little boy smiled up at him, taking hold of his hand, a new warmth crept over him.

"Looks like the real Tara is back," Bill had remarked.

"Sure is," Jake agreed. "Only now she's Tamara again."

"She wouldn't have wanted to stay here, anyway," added Robbie wisely. "She likes singing too much...and JJ."

Jake ruffled his son's hair. "And you're all right with her going?"

Robbie had simply shrugged in a matter-of-fact way. "I'm a little bit sad, but if I get that pony tomorrow, and my puppy, then I'll be too busy to think about it."

"Best get an early night then," Bill had suggested, and the little boy had been only too happy to oblige.

Darkness hung like velvet in the air as Jake strode purposefully along the narrow lane, thinking forward now. A sliver of moonlight peeped through a gap in the clouds, casting its pale beam across the ground ahead, and his heart lightened. The moonbeam felt like a sign, leading him to where he was supposed to go.

Jake had never felt more sure of anything

in his life than what he was about to do. He just hoped she'd be there. He had built himself up to this moment, and he hadn't thought to look past it.

When he saw her through the window as he walked along the pathway at the back of the house, warmth crept through his veins. She was nursing the ugly cat, gently stroking its rough fur while Puddle sat at her feet, halfway between sleeping and waking. Beside him, Bess whined and Cass looked up, peering through the window to see his dark shape looming. She jumped to her feet, obviously startled, placing the cat carefully back into its bed before hurrying to the door. He opened it before she reached it, basking in its bright warmth.

"Sorry, I didn't want to disturb you. You seemed so comfortable there."

"No problem." She smiled, a polite, distant kind of smile, as if he were a stranger coming to call. "Is everything all right?"

He stepped inside, his presence filling the small room. She placed her hand against her heart.

"I take it that's the ugly cat," he said.

A flush colored her cheeks. "He isn't

ugly, just neglected. Did Robbie say something to you?"

Jake smiled, reaching out to stroke the cat's rough fur. "Yes, your secret's out, I'm afraid. He told me what you said, too... about all God's creatures."

She glanced away and back again, unable to drag her eyes away from his.

"He comes over to see me sometimes. I was just trying to help him understand."

Stepping toward her, Jake took both her hands, unresisting, into his.

"And you did. You did help him...more than you know."

"He's a great little boy, Jake. You must be so proud of him."

"Marry me, Cass."

She looked up at him, her eyes wide with shock and emotion.

"Robbie says your eyes are like warm dark chocolate," he murmured. "Please, marry me Cass."

"But what about Tara?" she began as panic set in. "And Robbie?" Had she really heard him right?

His answer was simply to draw her so close she could feel the heavy thump of his heart, as if it was taking over her whole being and beating for two. Rebellion flared and faded as she looked up into his eyes.

Slowly he lowered his face to hers.

"I love you, Cass Truman—that is all that matters. Please say yes because if you don't, I'll ask you again and again, every day for the rest of our lives."

"Then I'd better say yes right now," she murmured.

And as she drowned in his kiss, suddenly she knew—this was the moment she'd been waiting for all of her life.

* * * * *

LARGER-PRINT BOOKS!

GET 2 FREE
LARGER-PRINT NOVELS
PLUS 2 FREE
MYSTERY GIFTS

Love Inspired

Larger-print novels are now available...

YES! Please send me 2 FREE LARGER-PRINT Love Inspired® novels and my 2 FREE mystery gifts (gifts are worth about $10). After receiving them, if I don't wish to receive any more books, I can return the shipping statement marked "cancel." If I don't cancel, I will receive 6 brand-new novels every month and be billed just $5.24 per book in the U.S. or $5.74 per book in Canada. That's a savings of at least 23% off the cover price. It's quite a bargain! Shipping and handling is just 50¢ per book in the U.S. and 75¢ per book in Canada.* I understand that accepting the 2 free books and gifts places me under no obligation to buy anything. I can always return a shipment and cancel at any time. Even if I never buy another book, the two free books and gifts are mine to keep forever.

122/322 IDN F49Y

Name _____ (PLEASE PRINT) _____

Address _____ Apt. # _____

City _____ State/Prov. _____ Zip/Postal Code _____

Signature (if under 18, a parent or guardian must sign)

Mail to the Harlequin® Reader Service:
IN U.S.A.: P.O. Box 1867, Buffalo, NY 14240-1867
IN CANADA: P.O. Box 609, Fort Erie, Ontario L2A 5X3

**Are you a current subscriber to Love Inspired books
and want to receive the larger-print edition?
Call 1-800-873-8635 or visit www.ReaderService.com.**

* Terms and prices subject to change without notice. Prices do not include applicable taxes. Sales tax applicable in N.Y. Canadian residents will be charged applicable taxes. Offer not valid in Quebec. This offer is limited to one order per household. Not valid for current subscribers to Love Inspired Larger-Print books. All orders subject to credit approval. Credit or debit balances in a customer's account(s) may be offset by any other outstanding balance owed by or to the customer. Please allow 4 to 6 weeks for delivery. Offer available while quantities last.

Your Privacy—The Harlequin® Reader Service is committed to protecting your privacy. Our Privacy Policy is available online at www.ReaderService.com or upon request from the Harlequin Reader Service.

We make a portion of our mailing list available to reputable third parties that offer products we believe may interest you. If you prefer that we not exchange your name with third parties, or if you wish to clarify or modify your communication preferences, please visit us at www.ReaderService.com/consumerschoice or write to us at Harlequin Reader Service Preference Service, P.O. Box 9062, Buffalo, NY 14269. Include your complete name and address.

LILPDIR13R

ReaderService.com

Manage your account online!

- Review your order history
- Manage your payments
- Update your address

> ### We've designed the Harlequin® Reader Service website just for you.

Enjoy all the features!

- Reader excerpts from any series
- Respond to mailings and special monthly offers
- Discover new series available to you
- Browse the Bonus Bucks catalog
- Share your feedback

Visit us at:

ReaderService.com